*For all those who struggle with injustice —P. H. P.*

"[A] segregationist is one who conscientiously believes that it is in the best interest of Negro and white to have a separate education and social order." —GEORGE WALLACE, GOVERNOR OF ALABAMA

**1950 and 1941** *Classrooms for white and non-white children under the "separate but equal" laws*

# MILDRED

Garnet and I walk in the grass
alongside the road
to keep our shoes clean,
but Lewis doesn't care.
He's shuffling through dust
in the middle of the road.
Garnet's
hand-me-down lace-ups
have the most life
left in them,
so they're the best.
She gets the best
'cause she's oldest
and has the feet
to fit them.
I wear
her way wore-out saddle shoes
from last year
but painted and buffed
till they nearly glow.
To me, they're the best—
being saddle shoes—
even though I can feel every
stick and pebble
through the thinned-down
soles.
Lewis wears boots so wore-out—
looks like Nippy

chewed them soft
out in the barn.
Being the youngest
of seven brothers—
no telling who wore
those boots
before him.

Lewis is right down in the truck ruts
kicking up dirt and stones
onto my white polished shoes
till I have to say,
       "Just quit it."

So he says,
       "MAKE ME."

I say,
       "You know I can, Pipsqueak."
He's just eight and this is a truthful
description of his size.
I grab him around
his scrawny middle.

He hollers,
       "Don't touch me, you,
       you STRING BEAN."

He's laughing hard
'cause he knows I won't
really whup him
'cause I'm five years older
and five years bigger.

Now I'm laughing
hard enough I could just about
choke
but I manage to say,
    "Don't you EVER call me
    String Bean,
    you Pipsqueak."

And I yell to Garnet—
who's walked ahead
because she is just too old
for this nonsense—
    "Help me, Garnet."

Well maybe not too old
'cause Garnet comes and
grabs hold of Lewis's elbow
and I hoist the other
and we fly Lewis over
that dirt road
with him pedaling mid-air
and hollerin'
and that's how we arrive
at Sycamore School.

We are all in Miss Green's class—
Lewis at the bottom
in first grade,
so Miss Green directs him
to the front row.
Garnet's at the top,
in seventh,
she's in the back.

I'm across the aisle
being in sixth—
all in one room, one teacher
for everyone.

Miss Green hands each of us
older kids a sheet of paper
and pencil and says,
          "Put your name in the top-right corner
          and write what you did
          during summer
          vacation."

Didn't she keep
last year's report?

I write, "Mildred Jeter"
and my paper tears.
I lift it and see that
my desk is a very sad
excuse for a desk.
Carved into the wooden top
are initials—
J. J.—
which most likely was
dug out by
my much older half brother
James Jeter
and I bet he got a thrashin' for that.

And there's P. F. and E. J.
and even a heart with
R. G. and A. M., and I try
to figure which of
my brothers, cousins, or neighbors
belong to those initials.

But Miss Green says,
        "Mildred? Is there a problem?"

"No, ma'am," I say.

I lay my paper back down,
and no sooner set my pencil to it
when it tears again.
I lift my desktop to see if there's
more paper inside and there isn't.
Inside me
something hard and tight
makes me
slam that desk
shut.

"Mildred," growls Miss Green.

"Miss Green, ma'am," I say,
in my most polite voice,
        "This is a mess of a desk. It is
        all carved up."

Miss Green comes over and
hands me a reading book
with a broken spine, says,
        "Put your textbook under your paper
        and try again."

I take the book,
open it up
to see *Edward Jeter*
(another half brother)—
written sloppy
and then crossed out
and *George Jeter*

also written sloppy,
crossed out,
and plenty of other names
crossed out.
You'd think it would
be a comfort—
knowing my big old brothers
read these very pages,
these very stories,
but what I see is all those
many names—
CROSSED OUT.
I know my lower lip
is jutting way forward
the way it does
when I am peeved.
My eyes sting
so I suck my lips into
my mouth to keep
from crying.
My desk is rotten
and I want a brand-new reader
that smells like ink and glue
rather than this one that
reeks of grime and mildew
and has been in the
germy hands
of many boys.

At that moment,
Garnet leans across the aisle
and touches my wrist.

I don't dare look at her
or surely I will cry.
She hands me her paper,
I set it on the old reader
and focus on it hard
so I won't cry.
Still,
one tear plops onto the paper.

I write this (around the teardrop):

> *This summer vacation*
> *was pretty much like*
> *last summer vacation.*
> *Garnet and I galloped*
> *through the woods*
> *playing horses.*
> *I pulled weeds out from between*
> *the turnips, collards, and mustard greens.*
> *I piled straw around potatoes.*
>
> *The whole family went to*
> *Bowling Green for the carnival.*
> *I threw a ball, hit the bull's-eye,*
> *won the tiniest little doll*
> *you ever saw—no bigger than*
> *a clothespin, wearing gingham*
> *and an apron.*
>
> *Friends and cousins came over*
> *to our house.*
> *We stayed up late.*

My page is filled so
I just sit and daydream
while Miss Green teaches
the little kids their ABCs.

With so many brothers
I am grateful to have my big sister
Garnet.

We run up and down hills
climb trees
catch tadpoles with our cupped hands
from out of the creek.
Daddy and my brothers—
they hunt squirrels and rabbits
with a shotgun.
They fish for perch and shad
in the streams.
My mama cooks those fish up fine.

Our Jeter ancestors have lived here
in Central Point
for centuries,
hunting and fishing.
Daddy and Mama
are both part Indian.
We are also descended
from African slaves.
And their owners.

Our section—
our rolling hills and woods—
threaded with creeks
is the most beautiful
in the whole wide world.

Besides the greens,
last spring
Garnet and I
helped plant corn
string beans
and turnips
in the side garden.

We'll keep on
hoeing and harvesting
all through the fall.
We'll help with hog-killing
later this season.
Neighbors will come by to help
slaughter, butcher,
hang meat in the shed.

We all milk the cow,
make our own butter.
We wring the necks
of our chickens.
Mama can do two
at a time—
one in either hand,
holdin' 'em by their necks,
she whorls 'em around
a couple times—
they never feel a thing.

Miss Green says,
        "Scholars, hand in your papers."
Garnet turns in a page
so she must
have found another
sheet of paper.

Miss Green hands out math books—
the same text I had last year
but I'm further along,
tells me to read on page 265
and do the problems.
Turn decimals to fractions—
not TOO hard.
Garnet gets a different
old book, writes her name in it.
Miss Green explains
greatest common factors
and sets her to work.
At the end of the day
Miss Green says,
        "Good work, Scholars."
We put our books in our desks.
We never take them home.

✳

Come Saturday,
folks drop by
our house—
young, old,
and everything in between.
This weekend
the big boys come over—
friends of my big brothers.
Theo goes into the refrigerator
looking for food.
Mama shoos him out.
But then adults come by—
out comes
macaroni cheese

hot dogs
potato chips.
And one unfortunate chicken—
who didn't feel a thing
and who I plucked—
gets dropped
into the boiling pot.
When the chicken is cooked
we all eat.
The boys eat too, of course.
We ALL do,
crowded around the table
eating
talking
laughing.
Mama nods and
Garnet and I clear the dishes.

On a blue homespun napkin
Mama sets out
apple pie
still warm from the oven.
Garnet and I
carved out the worms, cored,
sugared those apples—
that is,
after climbing the tree,
shakin' 'em down
pickin' out the best—
Mama calls that
talkin' like a farmer—
shakin' pickin' laughin' talkin'
but aren't we farmers?
Yes we are.

Mama made that pie.
We all dig into our slice,
lean forward and say,
      "One two three" (all together)
      "WHAT A TERRIFIC CRUST."
Which is what
we always say.
And everyone
at the table knows
Mama won't make
the next pie
unless we tell her
how good this one is.
She grins.
Then we lean back
so full we can hardly stand it.
Till Mama nods again.
Garnet and I push from
the table and clear away
all the dishes.

Then another family comes by
and they got little kids.
So Garnet and I go into
our room
quick
and each of us
hides our doll
deep in the corner of the closet—
this is not the itty-bitty doll
I won—
this is my just-about life-size
baby doll.
My itty-bitty doll

is living in the woods
in a hollowed-out tree trunk.

Mama sends all us kids
outside anyway.
The boys play catch
but we girls want
to play kickball.
Home plate is the bare spot
behind the shed.
The old plum tree stump
is first base.
The gnarly apple tree
is second.
Third is the rock.
I'm up
and I kick the ball right
through the branches
of the apple tree.
One of the big boys catches it.
He's not even in the game.
He throws it to the pitcher,
she throws it to first.
Too bad, I'm already at second
on my way to third
but I yell bloody murder
at that big boy
'cause he's not part of our game.

Because of him
I don't get
home.
I backtrack fast to third.
He's laughing like a hyena.

The game's over anyway
'cause the grown-ups want to
play softball with us.
And that's fun.
So we cross over to the field
where there's plenty of space
and the tall grasses
are trampled down.
I'm on a team
with Daddy, Otha,
and two of my much older
half brothers.
What makes them half brothers
is their mama, Daisy,
she died.
And then Daddy married
our mama.
Anyway, Eddy and Button
and a whole lot of more folks—
little and big—
are on our team.

Garnet's on the other team.
She hits a high ball
and I catch it on the fly.
Sorry, Garnet,
you're out.

She yells,
        "NO-O-O" real loud.

But she's a good big sister.
She says,
        "Nice catch . . .
        String Bean."

I don't mind her calling me
String Bean.
Because she said
it was a nice catch.
And it was.

Still, we lose.
But the best is yet to come.

More and more people come over.
They bring food too.
When it starts to go dark
Daddy brings out his banjo
and starts strummin' and pluckin'.
So Theo joins in on his guitar.
Eddy, Button, Doochy, and Dump—
That's all o' my big half brothers—
They all play fiddles and mandolins.

Really they are
Edward, Richard, George, and James.
The Jeters always play music
in the neighborhood
and make jokes—
make people laugh.
And DANCE.

One of the fathers calls
a square dance
and everyone joins in.
Otha dances
Mama dances
Lewis dances.
I surely dance.
Some of the big boys dance.
Mr. and Mrs. Loving—
eyes fastened on each other
even when they've been passed
to the next person—
their names are
Twilley and Lola.
I love their names.
But we call them
Mr. and Mrs. Loving
of course.
And they pretty much are.

If I stop and watch
I see young and old—
Indians, Negroes, Whites—
all mixed together.

Everyone likes each other
in our neighborhood.
Everyone dancing
TOGETHER.

Whites and coloreds—
we go to different schools—
to different churches,
drink from different water fountains.
But our section is different.

My world is right here
in Central Point.
That's what it's called.
Central Point,
the center
of my universe.
My family.
My world.

# RICHARD

Saturday morning,
I was under the hood screwing with the carburetor
of my '41 DeSoto.

Ray drove up. Looked over my shoulder, said,
> *Your car it been loadin' up on fuel.*
> *I'd adjust that on the lean side.*

*Yeah, yeah,* I say. *That's what I did.*

He said,
> *It's the weekend. Let's go.*

So we drove in Ray's car over to Jeters'
to see Doochy and Button and the rest.
They was sure to have good food.

We ate, played some ball.

I caught a kickball that went flying behind their apple trees
and their little sister went bananas.
Seeing her catch on fire was almost worth the hell
Doochy fired at me.

I didn't mean anything by it. Just having a little fun.
I apologized to the kid, though.

Then on Monday, me and Ray were driving the hardtop
toward home.

Here comes the flashing red light,
the wheezing of that siren.

Yep, Sheriff R. G. Brooks.

Ray stopped, of course. Sheriff is the law.

> *Let me see your license, Boy.*

Called him *Boy*. Hell, Sheriff calls Ray's father *Boy*.

I saw Ray roll his eyes—but Sheriff don't see it.

Ray's license, it says "COLORED." Sheriff hates "coloreds."
Sheriff—nasty as anything ever been—
leaned in the car, saw me, said,
> *What're you doin' here, Son?*

Not Boy. I'm SON.
Thank God, not his.

*I am coming home from work, Sir,* I say, slow and careful,
so he don't misunderstand any part of it.

What Sheriff means is
Why is a white boy in this car with a colored?

We never went to school together—Ray and me.
Before he dropped out
Ray went to Union, for coloreds.

I went to Caroline, for whites.
Before I dropped.

I hate this bastard sheriff.
But I make him think that ain't the case.
No use having the law on your tail.

I said,

> *I was walking down the road, Sir, and my friend here*
> *he offered me a ride.*

Sheriff nodded his ugly mug, sneered like a toad.
Stared up into the air.

I looked over at Ray. He was seething, but got it all corked up
like he can do.
Sometimes.
Lookin' cool. Me too, I can be cool.

Me, I'm white, but my daddy,
he drives a truck for P. E. Boyd Byrd—
maybe the richest roundest jolliest "colored" farmer in the section.
In other parts, a white man working for a colored man—
that would be unusual.
But that's how it is here in Central Point.

Sheriff don't like this one lousy bit.
White man puts hisself beneath a colored man?
Workin' for him?
Worse than being colored, right, Sheriff?
'Course, I didn't say that.
Just thinkin'.

Sheriff looked like he was chewin' on his teeth,
kept turnin' over that itty-bitty license,
trying to figure out what mean thing he could do to us.
We wait quiet
while he walked back to his car.

To Sheriff Brooks there are only two races—
white and colored.
In all of Virginia, just two races—
white and colored.

We know Sheriff ain't done with us,
but he let us go for now.

# BROWN VS. BOARD OF EDUCATION

 MAY 1954

In **1951**, thirteen parents filed suit against the Topeka, Kansas, Board of Education, protesting the policy of racial segregation. The Kansas District Court ruled against the plaintiffs.

The parents appealed to the U.S. Supreme Court. In **1954**, the Supreme Court gave its verdict, banning racial segregation in schools.

## "WE CONCLUDE THAT, IN THE FIELD OF PUBLIC EDUCATION, THE DOCTRINE OF 'SEPARATE BUT EQUAL' HAS NO PLACE. SEPARATE EDUCATIONAL FACILITIES ARE INHERENTLY UNEQUAL."

—*U.S. Supreme Court Chief Justice Warren*, Brown vs. Board of Education *verdict*

Even so, it would be **MORE THAN FIFTEEN YEARS** of struggle and protest before the last American school desegregated.

# MILDRED

I like Union High School okay.
I did eighth grade here,
now I'm a freshman.
Garnet's a sophomore.
If Otha hadn't gone and dropped out
he'd be a junior.
Theo dropped too.
My brothers'd rather work.
ME,
I'd rather study civics
science
history
English
even math.
I am surely going to graduate.

Union High School is
a far cry from Sycamore's one room.
It's a real school with classrooms
and a different teacher
for each subject.
I like walking from class
to class.

Each school day this week
after it's gone dark,
Theo, Doochy, and Dump
come home dog tired

after a day of helping
the Fortunes—
our neighbors—
killing hogs.
They're spattered with blood
and they smell pretty much
like hogs themselves.
Mama won't let them in
the house
till they first wash
out by the well.
What it comes down to?
They'd rather smell like pigs
than go to school
I guess.

The weekend comes,
we all go down the road a piece
over to Fortunes'.

When it starts getting dark
Daddy pulls out his banjo,
my brothers take out
their guitars, mandolins
and all set to playing
hillbilly music.
No one calls a square dance this time
so we just sort of dance around
doing steps, turns, and dips.

When they take a break,
Percy Fortune pulls an electric cord
through the back door
and sets down a record player

on the back stoop.
He lowers the arm and
out blasts
"Rock Around the Clock."

I set to dancing with my brother Otha.
Garnet dances.
So do lots of other people.
But after a few tunes
only Otha and me are still hoppin'.
We dance CRAZY.
He swings me out and reels me in.
My skirt swirls.
I throw back my head and laugh.
Someone says,
        "Look at that String Bean dance."
I don't even care.
Nope, not at all.
I know the boys are looking at me.
Sometimes that would be embarrassing
but not tonight.
I'm on FIRE. Happy.
Otha and I dance
tune after tune
until we are dripping
sweat.

When some folks start leaving
one of my brothers' friends,
Richard, says to me,
        "I'm drivin' you home."

I feel this rush of heat
rise up my already-steaming face.
He's sending me home?
Have I done something bad?
Then I think,
Well, who do you think you are?
Ordering me home.
Those thoughts all happen
in one quick flash
and I blurt out,
        "Well, is that right?"

But Otha is there, saying,
        "Come on, Millie.
        He's driving us all home."

Oh. Okay, well that's different.
On the way to the car,
Richard says,
        "Millie, sit in the front."

I sort of drop my jaw
'cause I don't like being ordered around.
When I look at Garnet
she shrugs and kind of grins.
When we get to the car
Mama says, "HURRY UP girls,
        let's get going."
Mama on Daddy's lap,
and three boys all stuff themselves
in the back.

I push Otha in ahead of me,
climb on his lap
and Garnet squeezes in,
we shut the door.
Richard gets in and we take off.

He looks at me
where I'm sitting
real close to him.
I look away and invent
something to say to Garnet,
      "Wasn't it fun dancing?"
She gives me a funny smile
and says,
      "Yeah it was."

It doesn't take long to get home
and we all kind of pop
out of the car it's packed so tight.
They get their instruments
out of the trunk.
On my way into the house
I look behind and Richard
is grinning at me.
I turn around quick
and go inside
and let the screen door
slam.

Garnet and I only have energy
to splash our faces
before rolling into bed.
I'm facing the edge
but Garnet's facing in
so I hear her whisper.
I think she says,
        "He's cute, Millie."

        "What?"

She says, "That sandy hair?
        He's strong.
        Taller than you.
        He likes you."

        "Who?"

"Pfff." She kind of poofs.
        "Who do you think?"

"Richard Loving?" I ask.

        "Yeah, Richard Loving.
        You're just being shy.
        He's nice."

        "Isn't he pretty old?"

"Not that old. Maybe Theo's age.
He works, laying bricks.
What's wrong with that?"

I don't say anything
'cause I'm thinking.
And Garnet goes on.
        "You were pretty snotty
        to him.
        He even thinks
        that's cute."

        "How do you know?"

        "I can tell."

Garnet has had boyfriends.
She knows these things.

"You should be nicer to him,"
she says.

I'm thinking about that,
and I want to ask Garnet
something—I don't even know what.
I just want to keep her talking.
But I can tell by her breathing
she's asleep.

# RICHARD

Saturday morning, wasn't in no mood to work on my car.
Wanted to find some reason—any reason—
to go over to Jeters'.

By and by, Ray drove up with Percy—
Otha, Doochy, and Theo in the back—
said, *Hop in.*

Good deal. I could maybe ask Otha about his sister. Or Doochy.
Otha might be better.
But I had to do it right.

Ray drove for a piece
then turned direct into the woods,
slid his old Chevy right over some brush,
turned off the motor
deep in the green
so the car was completely hid from the road.

We all got out,
followed Ray single file along a deer path
way back in the woods—
not saying nothin'.

I saw this big old oak we used to climb.
Shoot, we used to come here as kids.
We had a fort back here.

Ray said, *Check it out.*
Hah! Right here in the clearing,
Ray, he'd propped up an old pickle barrel on blocks
fitted it with copper tubing so it dangled in a copper vat.
What da' ya' know?
A STILL.
He was right proud showing it off.
He already done mashed the corn, sugared it
so's it was dripping clear as water
into a half-gallon fruit jar.

Ray said, *Purest moonshine in Caroline County.*

I said, *You son of a—*

*Watch it, Man,* he said, laughin' all goofy.

He sent around the jar.
Percy sipped, hooted, dragged his wrist across his mouth,
coughed,
said, *Yeah, that is fine.*
Doochy swigged, said, *Yep.*

I took a whiff. Smelled like it could take the finish off your car.
I took me a sip.
Turned aside and spat,
just barely missing Doochy.
  *That is* GODAWFUL.

They all laughed. The stuff was making them stupid.
They clapped me on the back.

When I could breathe again, I said,
       *This is honest-to-god rotgut. Got any beer?*

Ray said, *No, Man, this here is a moonshine party.*
       *Stop spittin' out my fine corn liquor.*

We was sittin' laughin' and someone, probably Theo,
told this story we all knew—
but Theo tells it real good—
about Sheriff Brooks
planting a gallon jar of moonshine
in old man Johnson's shed.
Everybody knows Johnson don't make moonshine.
He don't drink it, neither.

But Sheriff just walks into Johnson's house
like he walk into any colored person's house
without knocking
without calling,
and he picks a fight.
Old man slugs Sheriff, Sheriff arrests Johnson,
takes him to jail
then beats the hell outta him with a rubber hose,
saying, You use this hose to make moonshine?

Ray said, *Dumbass Sheriff,*
       *don't know you need copper tubing*
       *to make hooch—*
       *not rubber hose.*

But it ain't no fun being pissed off,
so everyone laughs—
at the dumbass sheriff.
Ray shook his head, called Sheriff some choice names.

I got home without asking about Millie.
I stood there thinking.
There was nothing to do but get in my car
and go on over there.

When I drove onto their stretch of gravel
Lewis ran out and said, *Let's drive into town—*
just when
Mrs. Jeter called out the window,
> *The boys are off fishing.*

Really? Fishing? Or sleeping off some moonshine?
I put my hands in my pockets
stalling.
I called out so anybody inside their little house coulda' heard—
> *I was wondering*
> *if y'all wanted to go to the drive-in tonight?*

*Sure*, said Lewis.
> *I wanna come.*

I heard mumbling,
chairs scuffing across the floor,
like maybe somebody pushed away from the table.

Garnet came outside.
> *Hi, Richard.*

*Y'all wanna go to the movies tonight?* I asked.

> *Yeah, sure.*

I stalled some more. *Uh, does Millie wanna come?*

*I'll see. I'll see who else wants to go. What time?*

*I'll pick all y'all up around seven o'clock.*

Someone called from the window, *Who is that?*
Must've been Millie.

*Richard Loving*, Garnet called back.
        *Wanna go to the movies tonight, Millie?*

A pause.

*Sure you do*, Garnet called back. *We all do.*

Millie still inside didn't say no or nothin'.

Garnet winked, nodded, smiled at me.
*I think she wants to go*, she said.

I drove off, doing little push-and-pulls
on the steering wheel
of my DeSoto
and ended up just nodding my head.
She wasn't making this easy.
But maybe she was just shy.

# MILDRED

I cannot believe it.
     "Garnet, why'd you do that?"

     "'Cause I wanna go
     and he wants you to go.
     You know you wanna go."

I don't know any such thing.
Everything I've said
points to, NO, I DON'T
WANT TO GO.

But maybe—
just maybe—
I do—
just to find out
if he's arrogant
like I think he is.

Richard picks us up at seven o'clock—
right on time—
in his green and white car
which is buffed shiny.

Otha
with our cousin Curtis,
and Lewis climb in the backseat.
I'm about to climb in with them
when
Theo and Doochy decide
at that last minute
that they're
coming.
They say,
      "Sit up front, girls."

Garnet pushes me
into the front seat
and climbs in behind.
      "Can we pick up
      my friend, Floyd?"

Which we do on the way—
in Bowling Green. So now
I'm squashed up against Richard
with Garnet on Floyd's lap
next to me
and the five boys in the back.

Richard says, "You look
      real nice, Millie."
And maybe I do,
'cause I worked on my hair
and I'm wearing a skirt and blouse.
So I say, "Thank you"
and,
      "It's real nice you takin' us
      all to the drive-in."

He's silent a moment
and the car is full of
conversation
and
laughing
which makes it easy
for us to talk
unheard by the others.
Besides which
we are smashed
very close together.
He says,
          "I asked everyone else,
          so you'd come."
He takes a quick look
maybe to see my reaction—
he's so close
I can feel his breath
brush across my cheek
and I wonder,
can he feel the HEAT
rising off my face?

He's older than me.
I feel all flustered.
I'm not embarrassed
when I'm with the
boys at school.
And really I've known
Richard
forever.
He's come to our house
since I was little.

He's part of the section
and the get-togethers
and we've all grown up together
only he grew up
five or six years earlier.
I decide to take hold of myself.

I say,
>"Well, I guess that's a good move,
>you asking everyone,
>'cause I might not've come
>if it was just you and me."

He takes his eyes off the road
right
when I take a look at him
and he's got
this big smirky smile
on his face.
I laugh and say,
>"Maybe you had better
>watch the road."

After a second or so
he kind of half grins and guffaws.

Lewis, from the back, says,
>"What you laughing at,
>Hyena?"

"Lewis!" I scold.

>"That's what we call him.
>That's what he IS."

Richard is smiling.
He's real good-natured.

And now there are lots
of conversations again,
and I release my
shoulders which kind of felt
tense and high
but I'm still watching him
out of the corner of my eye.

Richard is okay.
He doesn't talk a lot,
but he listens,
and gets a
quiet smile
on his face when someone says
something funny.
Sometimes he thinks
it's funny when no one else
gets what's funny
about it.

About a half mile
from the drive-in
Otha calls out to Richard
to stop the car
and unlock the trunk—
and that makes Richard smile.
He does what they ask.
Otha and Curtis
climb in the trunk.

There's a lineup of cars
at the entrance.
We hear the muffled voices of
Otha and Curtis
in the trunk
saying,

          "Hurry. We need air."
We laugh,
tell them shut up laughing
'cause they're using up
their oxygen.
When we get to the gate,
Richard, Floyd, Doochy
do the paying.

Garnet and I have dates.
We give each other a smile.

We drive through,
find a pretty good spot,
Richard gets out,
pounds on the trunk,
unlocks it,
and chortles as
the boys pop out gasping—
falling over each other
they're laughing
so hard.

They go up to the stand,
come back with RC Colas
and popcorn
for everyone,
then they climb
on top of the car with Lewis
to watch the movie.

We've got the sound box
hooked on the window.
Doochy and Theo
take off,
maybe looking for other friends.
Garnet and Floyd
get in the backseat,
and Richard and I
have the front.

The movie showing is
*A Star Is Born.*
It might not be the newest movie
but none of us has seen it.
Judy Garland is
so pretty
and her singing so BEAUTIFUL.
Garnet and I
love how Esther
(Judy Garland)
finds the guy in the end
who loved her
from the beginning.

On the way home
me and my sister sing
"Somewhere Over the Rainbow"
remembering how
Judy Garland was Dorothy
in *The Wizard of Oz*,
and the boys
are laughing at us
and we don't even care.

Doochy says,
          "Yeah, good movie,
          'A Star is Stillborn.'"

The boys,
including Richard,
crack up so hard
the tears are streaming
down their faces.
And yeah,
it is sort of funny
so Garnet and I laugh along too.

Richard has so many laughs
I have to find other words
for all of it—
chuckling, chortling,
snorting, cackling—
let's see—
cracking up, guffawing,
HOWLING.
That's why they call him
Hyena.

He smells spicy—
I think it's his aftershave.
He's shaved close
so his face is smooth—
not like a baby's bottom—
but not like sandpaper
either.

He puts his arm around me.
In the movie
when Esther gets kissed,
I let him kiss me.
It's a nice kiss—
not my first,
but the best—
soft and sweet.

# RICHARD

Millie was the last one out of the car.
I said,
>    *I'll stop by next week?*
But I said it like a question, 'cause she don't like to be told.
She nodded.

I drove off, hitting the steering wheel
of my good ole green DeSoto
feeling just fine.

# MILDRED

**A FEW DAYS LATER**

—◦— **OCTOBER 1955** —◦—

On Sunday the family
had dinner together
like always.
No one dropped by
which wasn't
like always.

On Monday,
went to school,
came home,
did chores.
Percy Fortune
dropped the boys off.
Just my brothers.
No Richard.

Tuesday,
went to school,
came home,
started chores.

Washing greens at the well,
I hear tires on gravel.
Look up,
green DeSoto rolls in.
Richard slides out.
I say,
    "The boys still out workin'."

He stands there,
car door still open.
I stand here,
hands full of drippin' collards—
just lookin' at each other.
A smile creeps across his face.
He closes the car door,
walks toward me,
slow,
says,
        "I'm not here to see them."

I still stand here
not sure what
to say.
He says,
        "I'm here to see you."

When he's right in front
of me
I figure out what to say.
        "What took so long?"

And he starts some slow
rumbling in his throat
which gets louder,
rhythmic,
then breaks into almost
a howl
of laughter.
Like he can't stop himself
he reaches round my waist
but I don't think my mama
would like that
so I side-step him,

still clutching my collards.
I laugh
so he knows I don't
really mind.

✺

Very next day
I'm waiting on the steps
at school—
waiting for Richard to pick me up
like he said
he would.
Garnet and everybody else climbs
into Percy's car.
        "Comin'?" they yell to me.

I say, "No. No thanks, I'm waitin'."

They shrug and drive off.

Fifteen minutes later
I'm feeling foolish—
then scared.
After four o'clock—
almost an hour late—
Richard rolls up.

I get in—don't say a thing.
Richard says,
        "The boss stopped in,
        started talking 'bout bricks.
        You know, bricking."

I don't know what to say.
What I'm thinking is,
it's a long way home
on foot—
like fifteen miles or more.

Richard says, "Bean, I'm sorry.
        He's the boss."

I find words. "Yeah,
        I guess you couldn't help that."

He sighs, starts driving, says,
        "You afraid I wouldn't show up?"

        "Yeah."

He says, "Won't happen again,"
and looks over at me.
        "Ever walk home before?"

I say, "Nope, never walked home.
        Always somebody driving."

        "What if nobody picks you up in the morning?"

        "Then we don't go to school."
It happens.
There's always chores to do.

        "You angry at me?"

Not easy to be
angry at him—
smiling all crooked
the way he does.
He's got as many smiles
as he's got laughs.

Am I angry at him?
        "I don't rightly know. Yeah. No.
        Maybe I was worried.
        I know you didn't do it on purpose—
        to be mean."

I roll down the window all the way,
let the breeze blow
through the car.

He looks at me, says,
        "You look pretty, Bean."

# MILDRED

On Friday night
Richard and I,
with Garnet in the back,
go pick up Floyd
and we joyride.

     "Watch for the sheriff,"
Richard says,
then goes FAST
on the hardtop
and lets the wind
carry us along.

Floyd says,
     "You off your rocker?
     Sheriff don't take kindly
     to speedin'."

Richard turns onto our road.
The trees all stretch over the top
so we're in a tunnel.
Feel protected.
Rained earlier,
so the dust is settled.
I hang my head out the window
let the wind rush through me.

We turn around,
drive through the tunnel again,
back onto the hardtop
and drive into
Tappahannock.
I feel kind of like a queen,
in here
all safe and comfortable.
Everyone out there
has to walk
in the street.

Richard parks the car
and now
we
are
walking
down the street.

Richard takes
my hand,
now we're
strolling—
makes me feel like
I belong
right next to him.

Floyd's got his arm
draped over
Garnet's shoulder
up ahead.

People looking
at them.
Or maybe not.
Maybe they're
looking at US—
Richard and me.
No matter.

# RICHARD

On my way over to Jeters' I saw Sheriff in a truck—
his dog in the back.
What was he doing on our road?
I want to tell him,
Get back to town. That's YOUR place.
Leave US alone.
But he just drove through slow, looking.
Patrolling, I guess.

Family already was playing music by the time I got there.
Millie was dancing with Otha,
looking real pretty.
But when the tune ended
she walked over to me, all heated from the dance.

We stood together. Close enough that
every now and then we touched.
Each time she brushed against me,
felt like I'd burn up—
but in the best way.

She turned to me, pulled my shoulder down
so I had to lean further toward her.
She whispered in my ear
which made me crazy—her warm breath in my ear.

She said my name. Just that.
Her saying my name sends me.
Saying my name AND whispering. Shoot,
I'm a goner.

# MILDRED

Hog slaughtering time.

We sugar-cure pork—
with more salt than sugar—
so we can trade
bacon and hams
at Byrd's store
for flour and salt—
also rice and sugar.
I missed a bunch of school.
The farm is important.

Neighbors come by and help
with the work
so 'course, we get together
on the weekend.

While Daddy
and my brothers
play music,
I take Richard
by the hand.

    "Come on."

I lead him to the woods,
toward the creek
where I've played
my whole life.

Richard and I
are protected by the dark.
Hearing my family's music
makes me feel safe.
I feel DARING
in the woods tonight.

I find a particular
old oak tree,
reach up into the hole
and pull out
my clothespin doll
that I won at the carnival
years ago.
The cloth of her dress
is browned and brittle.
Her face has faded.
I show her to Richard.
        "She's lived in this nice
        oak house for years."
I want him
to know my secrets.

He smiles
like he gets it.

# RICHARD

No one else at Jeters' wanted to see a movie
so it was just the two of us,
which was fine by me.

We headed for Daw Theater in Tappahannock.
Damned if we don't see the sheriff sliding by
like a snake
right when we turn onto the hardtop.
It's like he's everywhere.
But we're going the other way.

I bought tickets,
Millie headed for the side entrance.
Oh, right.
I seen movies from the balcony before
upstairs with Millie's brothers.
Percy Fortune.
Ray Green.
But not in a long while.
Up the dark stairs, one flight, another, another—
the higher we went the more it smelled like piss.
Millie saw my face all screwed up—disgusted-like.

She said, *Colored bathrooms don't always work.*
She shrugged, *Women's toilet doesn't always flush.*
   *They say the men's is worse.*
   *No one likes to use them.*

*But* and we're still climbing stairs,
  *they should take care of their business*
  *at home.*

I tucked her arm in mine, pulled her close
feeling her warmth.
We watched *East of Eden.*
Two brothers, Cal and Aron,
can't do nothin' but fight—
might as well be Cain and Abel.

Take it easy, I wanted to tell those brothers.
Life don't have to be
so difficult.

Maybe life is complicated when you have a brother.
But I don't see it in Millie's brothers—
all that sadness? No way.

Best part was the cartoon.
No.
Best part was my arm around Millie for a couple hours.

# SENATOR HARRY F. BYRD, SR., OF VIRGINIA CALLS FOR "MASSIVE RESISTANCE" TO SCHOOL INTEGRATION

 FEBRUARY 1956

Protesting the *Brown vs. Board of Education* ruling that segregation of schools was unconstitutional, Byrd and other southern politicians began a campaign to undermine and resist integration.

In the following two years, they signed into Virginia law measures that made it possible for counties to close public schools—even whole school districts—rather than allow black students and white students to share a classroom.

In one county, **ALL PUBLIC SCHOOLS WERE CLOSED FOR FIVE YEARS**.

"WHETHER VIRGINIA'S HIGH SCHOOLS, WHICH CLOSED ON A SEGREGATED BASIS, ARE EVER REOPENED ON AN INTEGRATED BASIS, OR INDEED EVER REOPENED AT ALL, WILL DETERMINE WHAT HAPPENS IN THE REST OF THE SOUTH. ONCE AGAIN, VIRGINIA IS THE BATTLEGROUND."

—*Edward R. Murrow, reporting for CBS*

# MILDRED

Missed a lot in the fall
but I'm going
to school
steady now.
Didn't see Richard for awhile.
I missed him.
But he's coming steady again,
picking me up after school
sometimes.
Taking me home.

This beautiful spring day
he says, "After everyone goes to bed,
     sneak out of the house,
     come down the road,
     meet me at the oak tree—
     you know the one.
     I'll be there at midnight
     waiting for you."

I wait for Garnet to snore her
soft little snore.
Everyone else has been asleep for ages.
I stay awake counting my breaths.
I pull on my pants
tiptoe down the stairs
carrying my shoes,
avoiding the places I know squeak,

pass my parents' room,
out the door
and I step into my shoes.

The stars sparkle.
The grass is wet.

I get to the road
and tear down it.
I hear an owl hoot
in the woods and
the flutter of leaves,
some squawks,
cackles,
the cry of some animal
who just lost
to another—
coming from the field
across the street.

The night belongs
to the animals.

It could be scary,
but any scariness
goes into my
running.
The dark of the night
is protecting me,
making magic.

I'm nearly at the oak when I hear
an owl hoot
right nearby.

I startle.
Richard comes
out of the woods.
Richard is the owl,
and now he's
FLYING
alongside me.

We're not laughing—
just breathing together.
He grabs my hand
and guides me to the car.
We get in
still don't say a word—
just breathe.

He drives to another spot
further down the road
and pulls
right into the woods,
so the car is
hidden
from the road.

We get out
and pick our way
through the woods—
brambles and twigs
snagging
at our clothes.
Then we're on a path
where Richard pushes
me ahead
and he trots behind.
You can hear
a million chirping
tree frogs,
the low moan
of a bullfrog.
Must be a creek nearby.

The night might belong to the animals
but it's ours too—
Richard's and mine.
I've never loved to run.
But TONIGHT
I could run all night long.

We break into a clearing
with a creek running through.
Richard pulls me into his arms
and I snuggle

under his chin.
The night is cool
but we are steamy.
A small breeze
tries to dry
the damp off our skin—
tries to cool
the impossible
heat.

I slip off my shoes
roll up my pants
and wade in
the icy water.

Richard follows me in.
I flick a little water at him
with my fingers.
He flicks back.
Just a little.
We're laughing.
He takes my hand
and we're
on the bank
sitting on a thick log.

Richard kisses
the top of my hair
my ear
my collarbone
my shoulder
then my mouth.
We're still breathing from
all the running
and because
we

are
JUST
breathing.
Until we're
breathless.
And
gasping.

We pull on our shoes,
take hands
and make our way
back to his car,
drive to the oak
where he lets me out. I sort of gallop
along the road
like when I was
a kid
playing horses.
When I get to my house
just as I reach the door
his car passes by
real slow.
I tiptoe upstairs
take off my pants,
carefully crawl into bed
alongside my sister,
let my
breathing
slow down,
not touching her
with my hot sweaty
self.

Richard and I
never said a word.

# RICHARD

Millie and me went to the drive-in up in Fredericksburg.
Ray and Annamae came along.
Garnet and her boyfriend too.
The car was packed and it being cold out
that night,
we really steamed up the windows.

Saw *Ain't Misbehavin'* so we all joked about whether we was.
Bean said,
> *I don't think you are misbehavin'*
> *if you love the one you're with.*
She's right.
And I'm the one she's with.

She takes her hand in just such a way, pulls her fingers
through her hair
to take the curls off her forehead.
And I fire up like a SPARK PLUG.
Just seeing her hand move through her hair.

# MILDRED

Outside our neighborhood—
like in Bowling Green—
some people look at us
and SCOWL.
If Richard sees it
he holds my hand tighter.
After they pass by
he'll lift my hand,
kiss it and say,
          "Caramel."

Tappahannock's carnival
is bigger and better.
Here we won't
see so many folks we know.
The air is sweet with cotton candy
and salty with popcorn.
We hold hands,
swinging our
clasped fists.

I say, "Let's go on the octopus."

Richard isn't crazy
about fast rides
but I love them.
So he has to be brave.

We get squished together
careening, soaring.
I scream.
He laughs
of course.
I know he did this for me.

When we're on solid
ground again
he says,
   "YOU'RE the brave one."

Sometimes we don't hold hands
just so people don't stare.
But sometimes—
SOMETIMES—
you just have to hold on.

Richard puts his arm around my
shoulders,
pulls me close
for a kiss,
and some fool
passing by
says,
   "Nice piece o' colored ass."

Richard tenses up—
balls up his fists—
like maybe he's even gonna
haul off
and slug the guy.

I pull him away.
Pull hard—
drag him away
really
till we are running down
the street and
laughing
again.

It's not like it happens
all the time—
cruel people.
The drive-in is good
'cause no one can see us.
And we always fill
the car
with family and friends.
It's like taking
Central Point
with us to the movies.

Richard once said,
        "It could be worse, Bean.
        If you was the white one
        and I was the colored one,
        people saw us together?
        They'd lynch me.
        We can do this."

I'm not real dark—
'bout the color of a grocery sack—
and I have good hair,

but I surely
couldn't
pass.
There are plenty of people
from our section,
who are mixed like I am—
and one day,
when they're grown,
they leave home
and never ever
come back.
And we know they
passed
into white society—
away from
where everyone knows you,
where everyone truly
cares about you.
I feel sorry for them
who pass—
and don't come
home.

# 1956–1957

"What good is it doing to force these situations when white people nowhere in the South want integration? What this country needs is a few first-class funerals."

—GEORGE WALLACE, GOVERNOR OF ALABAMA

**1956 to 1957** *Black teens attempt to attend previously all-white schools*

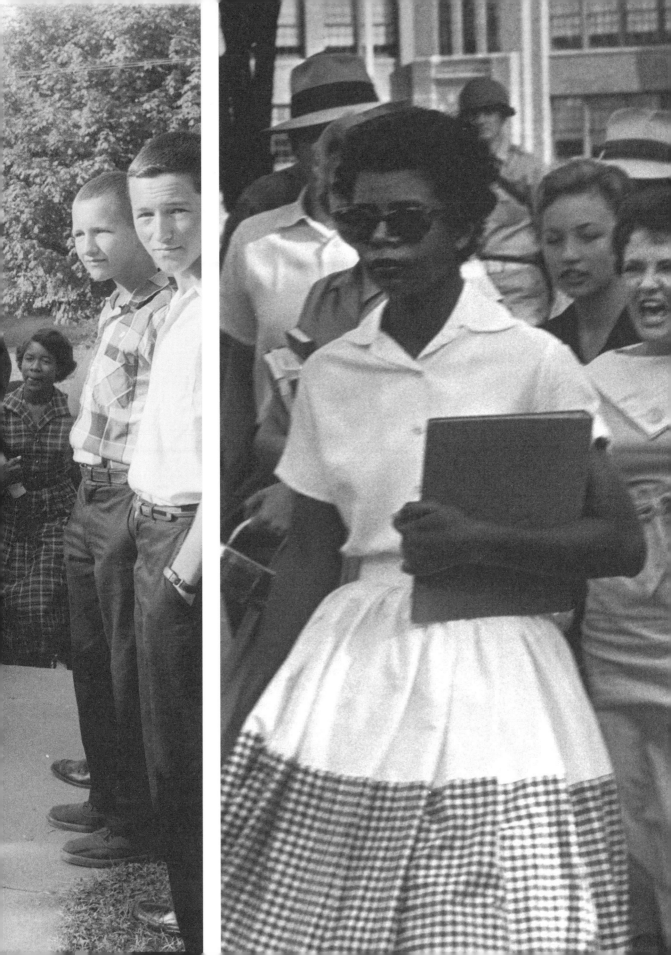

# MILDRED

I sit in class,
but I don't care about
*Great Expectations.*
I don't care about graphs.
I don't care about the three branches
of federal government.

I'm thinking
the longer I wait,
the worse this is.
No matter how much I jump up and down,
stand on my head,
grip hold of my guts and press,
this isn't
going
away.

Oh God Oh God.
Please.
I don't know what to do.
I haven't even told
Garnet.
She'd say,
        "I told you so."

Ignoring it
didn't make it go away.

Wishing it wasn't there
didn't make it go away.
I don't want this.

What will Richard think?
What will Richard do?
I don't want to lose Richard.

I can't go to the midwife
and ask questions—
find out what I might do—
'cause the midwife
is Richard's mama.

This is bad.
I don't show much.
I can still change into my gym suit,
take a shower with the other girls,
no one's going to see,
but for how much longer
is that going to be true?
I can feel the difference.

I am so scared
I sweat all the time
and even my sweat
smells different.
I sit in English,
and we discuss Pip.
Does he want to be
poor, ignorant, immoral?
That was a century ago.
In England.
I don't *care*.

I'm thinking
the girl in back of me
the boy in front of me
can smell
my fear
my difference.
They'll know.

I'm in trouble.
What
What
What am I going to do?

Oh Lord, help me.

# RICHARD

I drove up to Ray's. He's got my DeSoto up on blocks,
says, *Wanna race this heap?*
  *Take off the bumper, lighten it up?*
  *Percy can drive it. Over at Sandbridge?*
  *You in?*

I said, *Yeah, sure.*

His place looks more junkyard than anything else.

I said, *You oughta' clean this place up.*
  *You're a fine mechanic.*
  *You could make yourself a living.*

Ray shrugged.

It's time Ray settled down, acted more responsible.

I said, *Me and Millie going to Sparta dance tonight.*
  *You coming?*

  *Sure.*

# MILDRED

Richard still doesn't know.
I can't tell him.

Saturday night,
Daddy and my brothers
are the band
for a square dance
at Sparta School—
the elementary school
where Richard went—
the white school.
Colored people
aren't allowed in.

Light and music
spill out the open door.
Me and Richard are milling around
with a bigger group of coloreds
outside
where we're allowed
to listen
and dance
if we want.

Richard and his
car buddies,
Ray and Percy—
and Ray's girl,
Annamae—
are with us.
Ray, Annamae, and Percy,

being colored,
aren't allowed in, either.

White guys
with white girls on their arms
say
"Hey" to Richard
on their way in.
He "heys" them back.
Everyone likes Richard.

He says to me,
          "Let's go in.
          They won't mind."

          "We can't go in there.
          I can't go in."
I giggle
'cause I think he's kidding.
But he's got his arm
around my shoulder
walking toward the door
and he's a whole lot stronger
than me.

As we step into the doorway
a white man,
maybe the guard,
puts out his hand—
bars our path.
He looks at Richard
and cocks his head at me—
like
that says it all.

I know I'm not allowed,
I feel embarrassed.
HUMILIATED.
I don't care if I go in.
I don't like to rock the boat.

"You go in, Richard," I say,
my voice rising.
        "You wanna dance?
        You go in.
        You wanna listen to the music?
        You go ahead."

I feel my lower lip jutting out.
That's how I know
I'm angry.
I train myself not to be angry.
So I don't always know that I am.

Anger takes energy
that I'd rather use
being happy.
But now I'm ANGRY—
and I'm angry
at Richard.

I don't want to cry,
but I feel my lower lip
trembling—
my face is warning me
that the tears could start
spilling.

Richard knows me well
enough
to know this too.

He pulls me back
out of that lit-up
doorway,
out to where it's dark,
away from the people.
He puts his
arms around me
and he kisses my eyes
which are salty with
escaped tears.
He says,
       "Bean,
       Bean, I'm sorry,
       but your Daddy is playing in there
       and Doochy and Button,
       and all of 'em, Theo,
       and I thought maybe
       they'd let us in.
       It was stupid.
       I was stupid.
       Let's hang out here.
       It's nicer out here,
       in the dark,
       anyhow."

And Richard,
who never ever
dances,

just holds me
and we rock together
taking little steps
and we're
dancing.

The moment they said,
No, you can't go in,
he saw—
I know he really saw—
what it is
to be colored.

It's true—
when we go to movies
we have to sit up in the balcony.

But this is different.
YOU CANNOT
COME IN
HERE.

We walk to where
the car is,
climb into
the backseat
with no one around.

I tell him.
I tell him everything.
He's gonna find out anyway.
I cry while I tell him.

His face folds up
He steps out of the car.
I wail.
He's gone what feels like
forever
in the dark.

I'm in the car whimpering.

He comes back.

Drives me home.

# RICHARD

Had a bad night with Millie
last night. I just gotta think.
Don't know what to do.

# MILDRED

When the pains get bad
and close together
Mama sends Lewis over to Lovings'—
not for Richard—
for Mrs. Loving.

Lola Loving comes right over.
Mama is already boiling water.
I'm in the downstairs bed
on an old sheet and towels
that have been boiled
many times
for many births.
Lola says,
          "Push, Honey.
          You're doin' real good,"
over and over.

I'm crying
and Lola is saying,
          "The baby's coming.
          Push, Honey.
          You're doin' good."

Good?
I'm doing good?
What is good?

I'm screaming.
My mama sets behind me
propping up my back.
        "The baby is coming.
        Push."
The baby is here.
Lola puts the baby
on my belly.
And my mama
lets me lie back.
I cry.
Everyone cries.

Lola says,
        "You did real good,
        Millie. You're
        the right age
        to have a baby."
Young.
She trying to make me
feel better?
        "That was an easy
        labor,"
she says.

He's a wrinkled little guy—
looks like a little old man—
a Sidney.
I name him
Sidney Clay—
he's beautiful.
I love him.

# RICHARD

I drove up to Millie's. No one was outside.
I knocked on the door. Her mother came,
said, *Richard!* surprised.
She said, *Millie's napping,* then stepped aside
so I could see into the front bedroom.

It was dim inside because there's no window
and no light on.
Millie sat up and rubbed her eyes.
She ran her hand through her rumpled hair.
        *Richard?*

I stood in the doorway blocking the light
so maybe she couldn't quite see me.
Of course she was surprised. She hadn't seen me in weeks.
In months.

My eyes adjusted, we just looked at each other.
She patted the bed. I sat next to her.
I was about to say something—I don't know what—
I heard whimpering.
Millie reached behind her, gathered a bundle
cradled it in her arms.
Pulled down a corner of the cover, said,
        *Sidney, this is Richard.*
        *Richard, this is Sidney.*

She looked down at him, cooed at him,
looked up at me still holding that look of pure love.
She's a beautiful mother.
How can I not love her? How could I leave her?

*I'm sorry, Millie. I'm so sorry.*
*If you want me, I'm back.*

I choked up a little.
Millie cried, but not making no sound.
Just tears sliding down her cheeks.

She nodded. Nodded for a long time. She handed me Sidney.
I hesitated a moment, but I took him.
*Cradle his head,* she said. Soft and gentle.

# RICHARD

Millie and me turned off the hardtop to our road
which people been calling
Passing Road.
You pass up north from where we are.

Siren and lights. Oh shoot. The sheriff.
Bean scooted out from under my arm—
scared.
I pulled over.

> *Don't be scared, Bean, we didn't do nothin'.*

Sheriff swaggered up to the window.

> *Yessir,* I said.

> *Can I see your license?*

I pulled out my billfold.
He stooped to look in the car.

*And who is this?* he asked,
but I had the feeling he already knew.

Bean didn't say nothing, probably tongue-tied,
so I said,

> *This is Mildred Jeter, Sir.*

*Can't she talk?* asked Sheriff.
      *Your daddy Theoliver? Plays hillbilly music?*

I looked over at Millie. Her jaw set hard. I could see
besides scared,
she was angry.

*Yessir,* she said, kind of like a mouse.
My Millie isn't usually like a mouse.
Made me mad.

*What's the problem, Sir?* I asked—still real polite.

      *Well, you didn't have your turn indicator on.*
      *Nor did you have your arm out to signal.*
      *Now, that's a law—*
      *to signal when you turn.*

I wanted to say, It's late at night.
There's no one else on the road.
Why would I signal?
'Course, I stopped myself
from saying anything.

He seemed to be having a good time.
He leaned in my window so I had to smell his lousy breath.
He said, *This is a warning.*
      *I ain't givin' you a ticket*
      *this time.*
      *Now, you take that little Negress home*
      *where she belongs.*
      *And you don't go breakin' the law again.*
      *Hear me?*

*Yessir*, I said. I hated calling him Sir—
the sonofabitch.
I wanted to drive off so his arm would get wrenched.
But he was quick
in how he stopped leaning.
I didn't need no trouble, anyhow.
And I didn't
want Millie to be in no trouble
either.

So I drove off gentle. I patted Millie's knee.
I didn't want her to cry.
I took a quick look over at her.
She was staring straight ahead.

*It's okay, Bean. We didn't do nothin'.*

# MILDRED

Mama says,
> "I guess you're serious about that boy."

> "Yeah, Mama, I am."

> "Bring him round to dinner."

Richard comes
for Sunday dinner—
one o'clock sharp.
Aunt Coree Johnson comes,
most of my brothers
are here.
Mama boils
chicken, collards, turnips.
I slice bread
we baked this morning.
Garnet fries last year's apples.
And we have rice pudding
for dessert.
The cream is from our cow
who I milked this morning,
eggs laid by our chickens.

Richard has sat here
many times.
But today
we have on the checkered tablecloth
because he is my special guest.

The table is heaped with food,
Sidney in a basket alongside me,
family crowded around.
Richard grabs my hand under the table,
at the same time he slips the napkin off my lap,
puts it on his.
Still holding his one hand,
I grab for my napkin.
But he won't let me have it.

I can't help but giggle—
having our own conversation
with no words
under the table hidden by the cloth,
while everyone else
talks over the top
of the table.

# RICHARD

Over at Ray's with him under some car
I found an old can of paint in his mess of a shed.
It was part solid, but there was enough liquid to whitewash
the board I brought.

I told him, *Decide what you want on your sign.*
      *I'll get the black at Blatt's.*
      *Time you set up business—*
      *stop bein' a bum.*
He laughed.
Me too, I laughed.

He said, *You woulda loved seeing*
      *me—your friend, the bum—*
      *outsmarting the*
      *jackass sheriff this morning.*

*No,* I said. *No, no,* but I laughed.
      *Are you off your rocker?*

*No, listen,* Ray said.
      *I'm at the junkyard this morning*
      *looking for some copper tube.*
      *Up drives Sheriff, says,*

*Boy, what you need with copper pipe?*
*I don't wait to answer.*
*I'm off and running,*
*ducking between trashed cars.*
*What?*
*He's going to arrest me for some copper tube?*
*They know I'm good to pay for my piece of tube.*
*But not now.*
*I dip into the woods and I'm home free.*
*I dodge blackberries*
*knowing he's gonna plow through,*
*get his ass raked by thorns.*
*He's never gonna find my still.*
*It's a wild goose chase and 'course*
*I win.*

I said, *Ray, you lost your marbles?*
*Lookin' for trouble?*
*Man, you are gonna find it.*
*Don't go messin'*
*with Sheriff.*

# MILDRED

I know how it feels
from last time.
No mistake.

I haven't told
Garnet.
She'll tell me how
stupid I am.
She'll say,
Why didn't you—
Why didn't I—what?
What could I do?
Richard's a man.
He needs to do the thing.
And I wanted to do it too.

But I'm the one in trouble.
WHAT am I going to do?
What will Richard think?

*Lord, help me.*

# RICHARD

I asked, *Are you sure?*

*Yes. Yes. It's been three months, Richard.*

*Could there be a mistake?*

It was just a question.
But she went nuts.
I seen her upset before,
but never like that.

# MILDRED

How could he ask that?

> "Richard, what are you thinking?
> Do you want to get rid
> of this baby?
> Of me?"

He pauses.

In that moment,
I don't breathe.
I look him in the eye.
All this time we've
been doing it,
doesn't he know
what could
happen?
What could he be
thinking?
That I'd walk away
and do this
alone?
Again?
I'm about to look away.

When he says,
> "No.
> No, Millie.
> No."

He takes hold of my two shoulders,
pulls me to his chest.
       "I want to do the right thing."
He kisses my forehead.
       He says, "Do we need to talk
       to my mother?
       Find out when you're
       going to have this baby?
       And make plans."

Oh, Richard.
Thank you.
Thank you.
Thank you.

# RICHARD

Ray said, *You can't marry a colored girl. Not in Virginia.*
       *You're white, Man. Did you forget that?*

I told him, *We'll do the marrying in D.C.*

He said, *For godsakes, Man, live next door to her,*
       *if you have to be big about it.*
       *Look at Farmer.*

In our section
white man named Farmer
set up his colored woman in a little house
and he lived next door.
They have a mess of kids.
Everyone knows, but no one says.
All his kids take her name and when they grow up, they
leave—
pass as white people.
Somewhere.
Away from here.

Farmer didn't want to rock the boat.

Millie deserves better.
I called Ray a pig. I called him worse than that.

*I'm just trying to look after you, Man,* he said.

I said, *You wanna help? Ray?*
        *What you can do is steer clear of Sheriff.*
        *He knows we're friends. Keep yourself outta trouble.*
        *That's how you can look after me.*

He said, *You're crazy, Man.*

I said,
        *You got your moonshine.*
        *I got Bean.*

Ray said, *You think Sheriff gonna let it go?*

        *He might.*

Ray can't stop. *You know it ain't legal—race mixing.*
        *And Sheriff, he's mean through and through.*

I didn't say nothin'.
But, yeah, I knew.

Ray said, *You are dreamin'. You been rockin' Sheriff's*
        *racial hatred*
        *a long time—*
        *pretending all y'all ain't no different,*
        *everyone the same.*
        *Race mixing?*
        *That ain't gonna slide in Caroline County.*

# MILDRED

Missed enough school
doin' chores and stuff,
I'm still a junior.

Doesn't matter anyway.
I'm five months pregnant,
beginning to show.
I quit school.
Don't say anything to anyone.
Just stop going.

| MILDRED | RICHARD |
|---|---|
| | |

Baby due in October.

                That's what my mother says—

*My* midwife,
Lola Loving,                Lola Loving,
she says,                she says,

                We are—
    "You seem to be very happy.        we're very happy.

    Every time I see you and
    Richard
    together . . .

                And we're together a lot.

    at home
    in a car
    anywhere—                anywhere—
    you're happy.             we're happy.
    You ought to get married."    We ought to get married.

*My* mama says                *Her* mama says we fit together.
    . . . that we fit together
    just right.

                Her head fits right here under my chin.

    "You grew up together.
    You know each other.        Yeah,
                we know each other.

    That's good.             That's good.
    You ought to get married."    We ought to get married.
So that's what we're doing.    So that's what we're doing.

                I found us a preacher
Who will marry us . . .        who will marry us
                at his house
. . . in Washington, D.C.?    in Washington, D.C.

We drive in Richard's car—
Mama, Otha, Daddy,
Richard, and me.
First,
at City Hall
we fill out the paperwork . . .

I drive

to City Hall.

I write,
Richard Perry Loving
White
from Passing, Virginia,
age twenty-four
marries . . .

to marry.
And I write,
Mildred Delores Jeter
from Passing, Virginia,
age eighteen
Indian—

          Yes, I'm Indian.

Indian? That's what you
wanna say?

Yeah, I know.
Okay.

On the second day of June 1958
Washington, D.C.
          And then I sign the paper.
My hand shakes a little
when I sign
my name.

Does he really love me?

On the second day of June 1958
Washington, D.C.

When she signs
her name
I smile at her.

The sheriff—
the government—
can't tell me who I can marry.
Or who I can't marry.

Or is he just
doing his
duty . . .

It's my duty to marry
the woman who is having my child.

. . . because I'm pregnant?

It's got to be done—
I'm marrying her.

I'm scared . . .
Richard?

Shhhhh. Everything's going to be
okay, Bean.

Okay.
Okay.

And then the preacher, at his house,
he asks,

*Do you promise to cherish him*
*to honor him*
*to protect her in sickness*
*and in health,*
*for richer or poorer*
*for better or worse*
*until death*
*do you part?*

*Do you promise to cherish her, to*
*honor her*
*to protect him in sickness and in*
*health,*
*for richer or poorer*
*for better or worse*
*until death*
*do you part?*

I do.

I do.

We kiss.

We kiss.

I put my hand on . . .

I wrap my arm around
her middle—
grinning like an idiot.
Can't help myself.

. . . my widening middle . . .

I smile up at him.

I kiss her hair.
I love her innocence—
her sweetness.

We drive on home . . .

She doesn't know we're breaking
the law—
stupid-ass law—
once we return home to Virginia.

. . . have a party—
just small.

Maybe they'll forget us—
leave us alone.
We'll be quiet.

We sleep in the
downstairs bedroom.

I promise to build her
a house . . .

He'll build me a house
across from my parents

soon as we save the money.
Right here.

right here—
our home.

Life is good.
I'm a married man.
I have me a beautiful wife.
We're going to have a child.

I'm going to have this child
and raise our family
right here
in Central Point.

And raise our family
right here
in Central Point,
home.

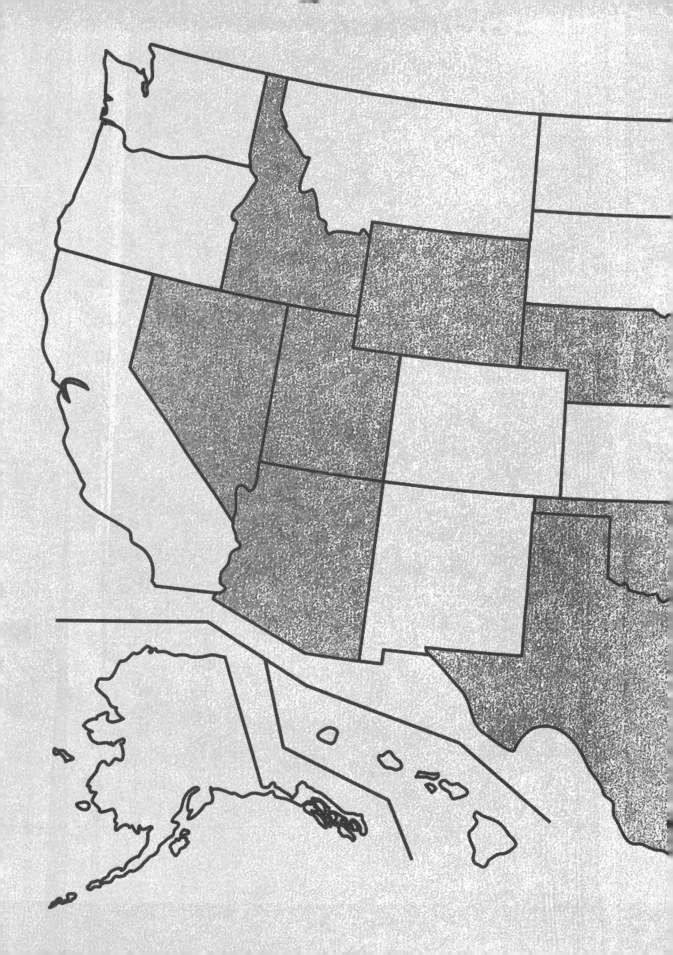

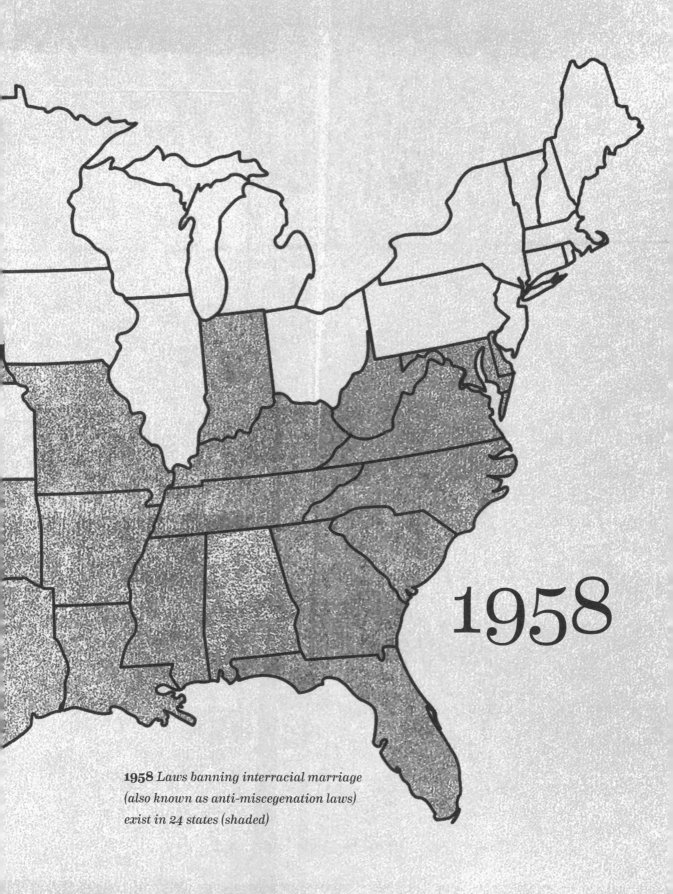

1958

**1958** *Laws banning interracial marriage*
*(also known as anti-miscegenation laws)*
*exist in 24 states (shaded)*

# RICHARD

Till we get our own house built,
I make myself scarce.
Lot of people in that little Jeter house.

Went over to Ray's after work.
Brought Millie with.
She went inside with Annamae.
Ray and me worked under the hood
of the Ford.

# MILDRED

Percy drives the Ford
out to Colonial Beach—
drives real easy
real careful.
Mama keeps Sidney, so
I can go with Richard—
along with Annamae and Ray—
in the DeSoto
which is running
real nice again.

Annamae and I
are in the stands,
the boys are down with the car
getting ready
for the next race.
Because we're talking excited,
guys in the stands
know it's our car.
Man asks me,
      "What's it got in it?"

"'Bout two-sixty," I say,
      "They bored out the engine,
      you know.
      "Annamae, you know exactly?"

      "What are you talkin' bout?"

"Cubic inches.
How many cubic inches?"

"You are talkin' Russian, Girl."

Annamae and I laugh
but I feel right proud
to know what the guy means—
what's it got in it?

Our car is stripped down
so it looks different
than a lot of the others.
We need to beat twelve seconds—
really eleven something.

Percy's up
against a souped-up Chevy.
They're both revving
their engines—
like roaring animals.
The starter guy holds two flags
real still
but they flap in the breeze—
then the red flag whips straight down—
FAST.
Percy presses on the gas
lets up the clutch
tires spin a second
car lurches forward
and they're off,
sitting on back wheels
like animals

like I imagine jaguars—
running smooth.
Annamae and me are up
screaming our lungs out.
Percy's in the lead.
But the Chevy's gaining on him.
The Chevy screams across the line
and the guy drops the flag—
then another.

It's over so fast.
Just a quarter mile.
I plop back down on the bench.

What's our time?

# RICHARD

We lost our heat. DAMN. We
won't be bringing home
no trophy
today.

# MILDRED

Richard and I go to bed
downstairs
on a hot sticky night—
nothing unusual
for a Virginia summer.
Sidney sleeps upstairs now.
Our bedroom door's open
to catch any little breeze
that might come along
to give us
relief.

I dream
the car engine roars,
brakes squeal.
You know
the way a dream pulls
sounds from the awake world
to make it a
dream story?
I realize later,
that's what I did.

I open my eyes
to a beam of light
shining through the window
in the hall outside our bedroom.

Then blinding light right in
my eyes.
I'm ready to scream,
but Richard
spooned behind me
must have woke up
and pulled me tight
into his body—
which stops the scream.

Then a cruel voice
right over me says,
        "Who's that woman
        you're
        sleeping with?"
I can't see who's speaking
what with the light in my
eyes.

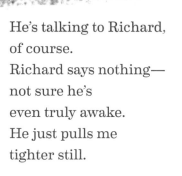

He's talking to Richard,
of course.
Richard says nothing—
not sure he's
even truly awake.
He just pulls me
tighter still.

"I'm his wife," I say.
It makes me feel brave.
I'm his wife.

Richard lifts onto
his elbow,
takes his arm away
from me
to shield
the light
from his eyes.

Richard points to the marriage certificate
framed on the wall
behind us.
Beam of light leaves our faces
to shine on the certificate—
so I can see it's Sheriff Brooks
and two deputies—
but I already knew that.

     "Not here, she ain't,"
says the sheriff.
       "Come on, get dressed,
       let's go."

I scurry up the stairs,
pull on yesterday's dress.
The whole house is awake—
Mama, Daddy, Otha, Lewis, Garnet—
no one says a word.
They don't dare.

Mama watches me go off
with the white men.
Get in their car.

Go to jail.

# RICHARD

I knew once we was married
and crossed the Potomac River back into Virginia,
Sheriff Brooks might get wind,
might come
arrest us.
I thought maybe if we laid low—
real low, kept quiet,
kept to Central Point,
he'd forget about us.

I couldn't tell Millie.
She was already moody,
what with being pregnant,
dropping out of school, everything.
I knew she was pretty innocent.
Innocence what got her Sidney—sweet Sidney.
Hell, I love her innocence.

We been married all of five weeks.
Took Sheriff just five weeks to find out,
make his move.
Maybe it would've been better
I told her.

Jail is a hellhole. Sixteen bunks in it.
Both white men and colored men here—
ain't no motel.

I wonder where they took Millie.
Won't let me talk to her.
Grabbed me rough the moment the car stopped.

Gave me a blanket,
shoved me in the cell.
I climbed into an upper bunk,
didn't sleep.
Eyes wide, wondering what's next.
Wondering about Millie.

Must've dozed, 'cause I was woke
and it was light.
Told me to come front.
My sister Margaret posted bail.
$1,000.
I owe her.

Millie's still there.
They said if I try to get her out
I go right back in.
They said,
>  *Don't expect the kinda*
>  *party you experienced the first time around.*

# MILDRED

I'm upstairs behind bars
in the only cell
for a woman—
just big enough
for a cot,
a sink,
a commode,
and one tall
pregnant
colored
girl—
ME.

We broke the law
by marrying,
says Sheriff Brooks.

Richard, he's out.
That's good.
But I'm scared.
I pull my feet up
best I can
under this growing belly,
off the sticky floor
pull 'em up onto the bed
so the rats
can have the floor
to themselves.
I breathe through
my mouth
so I don't have to
smell bug spray.

I never thought
I'd be in prison.

From high school
to wedding
to prison.

After two days
my mama comes to visit.
I try not to cry, but I cry
real easy these days.
Mama says it's the pregnancy.
I know that.
She says, "We tryin', Baby,
      but we don't want to rock the boat.
      They say we can't get you out
      or they'll punish Richard bad.
      You don't want that now,
      do you?"

No, no,
'course not.
Will they let me out to have my baby?
I can't have a baby in here—
with the rats
scurrying across the floor.
I CAN'T.
They must know that.

I been in here three days,
three nights.

They march
a man past me—
I'm the only girl here—

this white guard
marches this
white inmate
up the stairs
to my floor
taking some fancy route
from the yard back to his cell,
and the guard says to him,
> "I oughta send you in there with her tonight—
> with the Negress."

I know he's tryin'
to scare me.

I can hardly sleep,
keeping one eye open,
to see if anyone
comes.

Another day passes
and I'm still in here.
Mama comes to
visit again.
She says, "Daddy can't come
> 'cause, all I know,
> they'll throw him in too."
And not my brothers—
they can't come either.
"They're harder on men
than women," she says.
> "There's nothing
> we can do, Baby."
I don't want to cry again
in front of my mama.
She already feels so bad.

I ask her, "How's Sidney?"

"He's fine. Asked for his Mama,
but he's fine.
I can take care of Sidney."

I sleep on my cot,
wake up on my cot.
At mealtimes
food is handed
through the little window
cut in the bars.
I use my commode,
bathe in my little sink,
hold my belly close,
sorry this baby
been in jail before
it ever sees the world.
I live under the eyes
of my white guards—
those two deputies—
FIVE nights,
SIX days.

On Thursday,
my daddy comes
and pays my $1,000 bond.
Everyone we know
must have pitched in.
First I get pregnant,
get pregnant again,
drop out of school,
then I get ARRESTED.
I am so ashamed.

I don't know why they
decide to let me out.
I go home
to my parents' house—
the house where me and Richard
were arrested.
But I get to be with my Sidney.

Richard at his parents' house—
the Loving house.
They say,
        "Keep apart."
We surely do not want
to go back to jail.

Doesn't matter one hoot
that we married in
Washington, D.C.
Here
in Virginia
can't be married.
We're told it's true
in most every other state as well.
No race mixing.
That's what they say.

Our baby will be born
before the court date.

Me with my parents,
Richard with his.
We wait.

# MILDRED

**A COUPLE WEEKS LATER**

—◦— **AUGUST 1958** —◦—

I live at home
like I always did—
wake to bird songs,
hoe in the garden
while Sidney sits in the grass.
I shuck corn,
pluck a chicken now and then,
help Mama cook.

I watch sparrows feed
their new-hatched babies
in the gnarly apple tree.
For two weeks I watch—
and still
no Richard.

Richard isn't supposed
to come over.
We are living a lot of
suppose-tos.
But is he really not going to see me?
Is he relieved?
Bye bye, Bean.
Is that what he's thinking?

Garnet says,
        "Be cool, Millie.
        You just got home.

He doesn't wanna go back to jail.
And neither do you."

So I wait.
I play with Sidney.
I WAIT for this new baby to be born.
I WAIT for our court date.
I weed the string beans and turnips.
I hoe between cornstalks.
I knit a baby bonnet.
Sidney's the only thing that holds my mind.
I can't stop thinking,
WHAT IF . . .
What if Richard is done with me?
What if I have this baby alone?
What if I end up all alone?

One day, I'm out washing collards
at the well
like I always do.
When I hear a car.
I turn around slow
hoping I'm well hid
by bushes.
Once you get arrested
in your bed
it's hard to be easy.

But it's Ray Green's car.
And who should pop out
but my husband,
Richard Loving.
I stand, smile.
He smiles.

He cocks his head
toward the backyard,
and we meet behind the house
away from the road.

He wraps his arms around me
and lifts his chin
so I slide my cheek against his neck.
I remember what a good fit we are.
He pets me
all the way down my back.
He turns me sideways
and strokes my belly.

Tears seep out, slide down my cheeks
but they are happy tears
that wet his shirt.
We still haven't said one thing
but he's told me everything
I need to know.

Finally he says,
        "I'm not supposed to be here."

        "I know."

        "Ray just dropped me by.
        I can't drive here, Bean.
        If someone sees my car—"

        "I know."

By and by,
Ray drives right up into the yard,
to behind the house, yells,
        "COME ON, MAN."

I let him go.
He says, "I'll be back."
He climbs in the car,
hunkers down,
and they drive off.

# RICHARD

She's standing at the well
holding a bunch of greens
like they was a bouquet of wedding flowers
carrying my child
smiling at me
that deep warm
smile.
Any doubts I might've had—
like this being just too much trouble—
drifted away on the wind.
My country gal.
I am her husband.

# MILDRED

Mama boils water,
Lola Loving helps.
I know more what to expect
this time around.
Still, I scream.
Garnet has taken Sidney away
so he doesn't hear.

Lola Loving says,
          "Push, Honey. Push now."

I scream and push.
Scream and push.
Seems to go on forever.

          "Here it is. Here he is.
          A healthy baby boy."

The two grandmas
ooh and ahh.
I cry.
Everyone cries.
Because this miracle
just happened.
A baby is born.

"When will Richard come?"
I want to know.

Lola says,
        "By and by. Just be careful."

Richard comes that same night.
I hand him the baby
wrapped in a blanket.
"Go ahead," I say,
        "He's yours too."
He takes the baby and
what can I say about Richard's face?
Like a warm rain washes
away all the lines,
turning his face
soft and smooth.

        "What's his name?"
Richard wants to know.

"I've been waiting for you
to name him," I say.

        "He looks like . . . Donald.
        How 'bout Donald?"

Richard's right.
He looks like a Donald.
"Okay," I say.
        "Don."

He cradles our Donald,
draws the back of his wrist
soft as duck down
across the baby's cheek.
Donny doesn't even wake up.

Now the baby is born,
we'll go to Washington, D.C.—
the four of us—
and live with my cousin Alex.
We are a family now.
Who ever heard
of a nest of birds
flying off
soon as the eggs hatch?

Right before Washington,
I have my hearing.
They were waiting
for the baby to be born.

I stand before Justice of the Peace
Edward Stehl III
in the Bowling Green courthouse.
I am told I acted
"unlawfully and feloniously"
by marrying a white man.
Our lawyer, Mr. Beazley,
advises me to plead
NOT GUILTY,
just like Richard did
at his hearing in July.

No CHild is FREE Until ALL are FREE

1958

And then I go home
to my baby
and little Sidney.
You'd think that
they'd want
us to be married,
what with a child and all.

But it's our beautiful brown baby
that is the problem.
This perfect baby is the result
of race mixing.
This child is the very reason
they don't want us married.

# MILDRED

On weekends
Richard likes to lie on the floor
with the baby on his belly—
both of them napping,
Sidney toddling around them.

But weekdays
Richard drives ninety miles
to Caroline County
and lays bricks.
At least
he gets to be near home
while he's working.

Washington, D.C., is crowded—
where we live.
It's all we can afford—
shared with Alex and his wife.
Lights outside our building
shine all night
so you can hardly sleep.
Not just city lights
but city sounds—
sirens, honking, yelling.
Inside
the baby cries—
I get up and feed him,
keep him quiet so Richard can sleep.

I don't fit in this city
with its hard edges.
I long to lie on the soft ground
tucked into Richard
in one of the many places
I fit along his side
with the baby on my chest—
Sidney on Richard's—
looking up at the stars.

What with all the city lights
shining all night long—
the stars are washed away.

Tuesday morning we wake
to cars honking
rather than birds singing.
We set out
for Caroline County—
though I know there will be no lying
on a blanket
stretched out on the grass—
no looking up at stars.
Still, we turn on to Passing Road,
stop in to see his parents,
then mine—
just long enough to drop off
their grandsons—
then we carry on
to Bowling Green courthouse
for our trial.

Sheriff Brooks is here.
He's big and mean
with hands like hams

and a piglet voice.
I hear him squealing
to his deputy—
I hear him say,
> "There's the white trash
> and his nigger."
We pretend not to hear,
but surely it was meant
for our ears.

We stand before
Judge Leon Bazile.
He tells us we can have a jury trial
but our lawyer, Mr. Beazley, says,
> "You were married in Washington, D.C.
> Right?
> Richard is white
> and you are colored.
> Right?
> Is there any point in trying
> to have a jury dispute that?"

No.
Would a jury help us?
Not likely.
Outside our section
what Virginian
is going to sympathize
with us?
We are
race mixing.

This time Mr. Beazley
advises us to plead
GUILTY.

We are married.
We have a child.
We are a family.
Of this we are . . .
Guilty.

Judge Bazile pronounces our sentence—
we can spend one year in jail
or he'll suspend our sentence
for twenty-five years
provided
we leave Caroline County
and the state of Virginia
*now*
and don't return together
for twenty-five years.

TWENTY-FIVE YEARS?
Twenty-five years
without our new little family
in the backyard
dancing
to my brothers' music?
No family dinners?
No pies at the kitchen table?
I'm thinking,
in twenty-five years—
that's 1984.
I'll be FORTY-FOUR.
Richard will be fifty.
Sidney and Don will be grown men.

The judge asks,
        "Do you have anything to say?"

I'm fighting tears.
No, nothing to say.
I turn to Mr. Beazley.
            "Does that mean we can come back
            in 1984?"

He says,
            "No. That means your banishment
            could start over again
            from that moment.
            They would re-sentence you."

We pay our court fee—
$36.29 each—
we start toward the door
to head back to Washington, D.C.

Mr. Beazley sees just how sad
we are
to be leaving home.
He says
we could visit our families
in Caroline County
as long as we don't stay together
overnight.

We carry that whisper of hope
as we drive off
to pick up our boys—
then drive ninety more miles to
Cousin Alex Byrd's
hot house in our Washington slum.

# SOUTHERN POLITICIANS' "MASSIVE RESISTANCE" EFFORTS ARE THWARTED IN THE COURTS

## JANUARY 1959

On **JANUARY 19, 1959**, three federal judges ruled that closing schools in a public school system denied the displaced students equality before the law, and ordered that the schools be reopened.

On the same day, the Virginia Supreme Court held that Governor Almond had violated the state constitution by closing schools.

The battle for school integration was not over,

**BUT THE TIDE WAS TURNING.**

# MILDRED

Horns blast.
Breaks screech.
People fight.
Garbage
sets on the curb
reeking to high heaven.
Old gum stamped black
into sidewalks
dirties our path.
Traffic whizzes by
even on Neal Street
where we live.

How I miss walking
the lane to get the mail,
grass soft under
my bare feet—
listening to chickadees,
wrens,
sparrows—
all singing out their hearts.

Cousin Alex and his wife, Laura, are real nice,
letting us live with them
and all—

I mean we help pay,
so there's something in it for them.
Still, it's crowded
and who wants to
go outside
into this city
that is hardly
even on the same earth
as Caroline County?

Come the end of March,
I can't stay in this city
any longer.
We drive home to Caroline County
for Easter.
The babies will stay with me
at my parents' house
and Richard will go sleep
at his parents'.

We're having a good time,
with Lola and Twilley,
Richard's parents,
and his sister Margaret
at my parents'
playing with
our babies.
Garnet, Otha, Lewis,
Doochy, and Dump are here.
Oh, it's so FINE.
'Course other people
come by.

Ray and Annamae Green
and Percy Fortune.

It's like old times,
laughing and joking.
People are comin' and goin'
all day.

I collect some recently laid
chicken eggs
so we can boil 'em up,
color them
for a hunt in the grass.
Mama's here in the barn with me,
collecting a big ham
saved for tomorrow's
Easter dinner.

Jack starts barking up a storm.
We come out of the barn.
Oh no.
Oh no.
Sheriff Brooks drives up
in his black Ford—
got his police dog.
That dog, barking and snarling
looks mean as the sheriff.

I see Richard duck into the woods.

Sheriff says,

> "I know he's here.
> I see his car yonder.
> You are violatin' your parole
> and you are both under arrest."

"Mr. Brooks," I say
right polite,

> "Our lawyer, Mr. Beazley,
> says we can come, long as
> we don't cohabitate.
> I'm sleeping here
> and Richard's going to his parents'
> for overnight."

"Wrong," he squeals
like someone grabbed his piglet tail.

> "Judge Bazile says
> you cannot come into Virginia
> together."

Richard must've been
listening
and he comes up
behind
and puts his hand
on my back.

Sheriff already won the battle,
but he can't
stop fighting.

> "Y'all come with me.
> Don't you run away
> or I sic this dog on you."

We hand Don
to Garnet.
He's crying.
I'm crying.
Sidney's crying.
Mama picks him up.
I'm not bringing any babies
back to jail.

Richard and I go off with
Sheriff Brooks.
Otha grabs my wrist, says soft,
> "I'll go get Frank Beazley."
I nod.

We get to the jail
to be booked,
they say we owe
$200.

Richard and I look at
each other from across the room
with a look that says,
Where we gonna get $200?
I try not to cry
'cause it upsets Richard
to see me weeping.

Mr. Beazley arrives,
talks to Sheriff,
makes phone calls—
I guess to Judge Bazile—
does a lot of talking,
we're just sittin' on benches,
waiting.

Finally,
Mr. Beazley comes and says,
        "I'm real sorry, Mr. and Mrs. Loving,
        this was my mistake. I said
        y'all could come back,
        but I was mistaken.
        Judge says he'll waive
        the fine and jail time,
        but you gotta go home."

And he means
back to Washington
which is hardly home,
but we thank Mr. Beazley.
We are not going to jail.

Sheriff Brooks says,
        "That ain't no 'Mrs. Loving'—
        that Negress is Mildred Jeter."

We go collect our babies
and get on the road for
Washington.
There'll be no
Easter for us.

1959

**August 1959** *Protest against integration, Little Rock, Arkansas*

# 1959

"In the name of the greatest people that have ever trod this earth, I draw the line in the dust and toss the gauntlet before the feet of tyranny, and I say segregation now, segregation tomorrow, segregation forever." —GEORGE WALLACE, GOVERNOR OF ALABAMA

**September 1959** *White protestors march against school integration*

# 1960

**February 1960** *Sit-ins sweep the country for several years. In 1960 alone, more than 70,000 people fill segregated lunch counters, movie theaters, churches, motels, libraries, and parks in protest.*

# FREEDOM RIDERS

## MAY 1961

## 1956

In 1946, 1956, and 1960, the Supreme Court ruled that segregation on interstate and city buses—as well as in transit terminals, waiting rooms, and restrooms—was unconstitutional, but noncompliance with integration was widespread.

## 1961

In 1961, a group (mostly made up of students) calling themselves "Freedom Riders" began boarding public buses in mixed-race groups and traveling through the South to protest continued segregation.

In May 1961, members of the Ku Klux Klan firebombed one of the buses and attempted to hold the doors shut so that the riders would be burned alive.

# 1961

# RICHARD

I work pretty steady in Caroline County.
After a day's work
I sometimes stop in at Ray's—
look under a hood with him
before heading on home
to the city.

I can't be seen here
with my wife—
but sometimes I drive her and the kids
to her sister's house—
and I go with the boys
out to Colonial Beach
to race.

Sneaking around is a drag
but it's gotta be done.

# MILDRED

We've lived in Washington
for almost five years now.

Wouldn't it be wonderful
if we could live at home,
see family
every day?
And give birth in my own house.
But I have to be thankful
that I can go home
sometimes
and not get caught.

Lola Loving is a good midwife.
She knows me and my ways
which helps when
delivering a baby into
this world.

We now have three beautiful
children—
Richard and I—
Sidney, Don, and Peggy.
When Peggy was born
I got to go home
for a brief time.

I feared
being arrested
but I SURELY wasn't going
to deliver that child
in the city
where no one knows me.

I do confess
that the children and I
frequently
visit Garnet
in Battery—
one county over from Caroline
in Essex County.
Garnet's husband—
he works there at the sawmill.
Their two sons play with our kids.
Richard drops me off early
at the house
and goes and lays bricks
or works on cars with Ray Green
on weekends.
Come nighttime, he drives up the dirt road,
to Garnet's,
turns off the lights and the motor,
glides in
silent as an owl
under cover of dark.
Pulls the shades if we haven't done it
already.

He hugs me,
hugs the kids,
and never goes outside once he's in.

As time goes on
and Sheriff Brooks, a county over,
doesn't show up,
we live easier—
but still, we're careful.

The men go off to work
in the morning.
Garnet and I sip coffee
while the kids
play outside.
Battery is an itty-bitty town,
and the woods is a stone's throw
from the boardinghouse
where Garnet's family lives.

We keep an eye out the window,
watch the boys run wild—
shoving each other, falling, laughing—
like we all did
growin' up.

Peggy's just a little thing
but she can keep up with the boys
pretty good.
I'm sorry she doesn't have a sister, though.

The boys have moved off toward the woods
so Peggy toddles inside,
sits with her doll,
talking to her
while Garnet and I gossip
about cousins and friends.
But while Peggy is near
I won't say one thing
about being banished
from home.
She doesn't need to know
anything about it.

The more time with Garnet,
the better I feel—
except for the fear.
But Richard and I decided,
the visits are worth it.
I was just too miserable
trapped in the city ALL THE TIME.
After all,
Richard works most days
here in Virginia.
It seems only fair that I
come with the children.
Children should grow up
in the country
where they can be FREE
to roam and explore,
catch tadpoles
and kick around in the soil.

The other day
they brought home
a collection of little striped feathers—
white and brown—
so pretty.
I fear what happened
to the bird.

Richard and I wonder
every day,
Will Sheriff cross the county line
and come get us in Essex County?
Or send the Essex County sheriff
after us?
I do not want to go to jail.
EVER again.

# THE LETTER FROM BIRMINGHAM JAIL

APRIL 1963

"There comes a time when the cup of endurance runs over, and men are no longer willing to be plunged into the abyss of despair.... One has not only a legal but a moral responsibility to obey just laws. Conversely, one has a moral responsibility to disobey unjust laws. I would agree with St. Augustine that 'an unjust law is no law at all.' One may well ask: 'How can you advocate breaking some laws and obeying others?' The answer lies in the fact that there are two types of laws: just and unjust. I would be the first to advocate obeying just laws."

—Dr. Martin Luther King Jr., Letter from Birmingham Jail

# MILDRED

Today
Sidney comes screaming
into the house—
        "Don got hit by a car,"
he hollers.
Oh sweet Lord in Heaven.
I cannot move.
I hold him, let him cry.
I cry
but I cannot go
out that door
for fear of what I'll find.
I am frozen.
This city frightens me
every day.
But THIS?

I put Peggy, who is really too old for it,
in the playpen, which is really
just a fortress of raggedy furniture.
I know she can climb over
but I don't want her outside
to see—
Oh God, what will I see?
"Stay here, Baby," I say.

"Okay, Mama."
She is my good girl
but she looks scared.
She just saw her mama crying.

I follow Sidney out the door.
There is Don
sitting up in the street,
crying.
I see no blood,
no gore,
no car.
I cannot understand his words.
He's hiccupping great sobs.
I pick him up.
He buries his head in my neck
while Sidney says,
  "A black car hit him, pushed him over,
  and just kept going."

This could not happen
in Caroline County.
First, there are hardly any cars
driving up and down our gravel road.
Second, if anything like this did happen,
everyone knows us.
Some neighbor would
gather up Donny and carry
him home to me.
Not in this city.

I remember too well being trapped
in my cell
at Bowling Green jailhouse.

This apartment in this city
is a jail cell
to me and my kids.
I can't let them go outside to play
for fear
they get run over by a car.

At night my cousins and I sit and watch
the newscast on their TV.
Richard's not home yet
but he's probably on the long hot drive to get here.

They are planning a big event
right here in Washington, D.C.
for later this summer.
Dr. King will speak
about voting
and jobs for Negroes.
It's one hundred years, says the newscaster,
since the Emancipation Proclamation
was issued by Abraham Lincoln
and the slaves were freed.
But so many goals have not yet been
realized.
They are asking Negroes and whites to march
to the Lincoln Memorial
August 28,
for dignity, self-respect, and freedom.
And for HOPE.

I say,
        "I'd like to feel . . . hope . . ."
I'm not sure what I want to say,
but I keep going—

"... hope ... that Richard and I could live
at home
in Caroline County.
I'm real grateful to be here, Laura,
but I want to raise my kids
in the country,
where there's room to play.
Where they're not all caged up.
Where they're FREE."

Cousin Laura sighs,
says, "Write to Bobby Kennedy.
        He's the attorney general—
        he represents justice.
        He might help you.
        That's what he's up there for."

I'm a little ashamed
of all the complaining I do
when they've been so generous.
But I just can't go on like this.
She's right,
I've got to do something.
I want
to feel ... hope.

That very night,
using our dresser as a desk
I lay down a sheet of paper
and write on the top,
        *Dear Mr. Kennedy*—
and tell our story.

> *I am Negro and Indian,*
> *my husband is white*
> *and we cannot be married*
> *and live at home in Caroline County.*
> *Please help us if you can.*

I sign it

> *Yours truly,*
> *Mr. and Mrs. Richard Loving*

Here in Washington my name is Mrs. Loving.
That is one good thing about Washington, D.C.

# I HAVE A DREAM

"When the architects of our republic wrote the magnificent words of the Constitution and the Declaration of Independence, they were signing a promissory note to which every American was to fall heir. This note was a promise that all men, yes, black men as well as white men, would be guaranteed the unalienable rights of life, liberty, and the pursuit of happiness. . . . Now is the time to make real the promises of democracy."

—Dr. Martin Luther King Jr., "I Have a Dream" speech

**1963**

**August 28, 1963** *The March on Washington—250,000 people attending*

# RICHARD

Millie says I'm lucky
to go back and forth to Caroline County
every day.
I suppose she's right.
That's where people know my work
so that's where I get hired.
I don't have a choice.
The problem is
I'm going broke—
going ninety miles
at thirty-five cents a gallon
twice a day.

Millie wrote to the men in power—
the attorney general—
they said,
*Talk to the American Civil Liberties Union.*
So Millie wrote them too.

# MILDRED

When Mr. Kennedy's office said
write to the ACLU
in Washington,
I did.
I wrote,
>   *Dear Sir,*
>   *I am writing to you concerning a problem we have . . .*
And I told our story again.

In not too long a time,
a Mr. Cohen calls up on the telephone.
At first I get kind of breathless—
I don't want to make a mistake.
But he seems to understand our problem—
he doesn't accuse us of anything—
so I calm down.

He asks if Richard and I will to come to his office
in Virginia.
I tell him, "That is illegal—
>   us coming to Virginia together."

"I am so sorry, Mrs. Loving," he says.
>   "Yes, of course. I have a little office
>   in Washington, D.C.
>   We can meet there."

We don't have to pay him.
He'll do this work "pro bono"—
for the public good,
he says.

I say, "Thank you, Mr. Cohen.
        That would surely be good for us too."

I hang up the phone and I feel
a little shiver rise up my backbone.
I want to go home so bad.
I NEED to be home.
I feel brave and strong.
We can DO this.
We can go home.

# RICHARD

We went to the lawyer's little office—
nothin' fancy—
and talk and talk and talk.
He said something like,

> *I think we can win, but it will be a long process.*

> *More than a month? Why?*
> *We just want to live as husband and wife*
> *in Virginia.*

What is so difficult about that?

Mildred put her hand on my wrist.

Then he said,

> *If you were to go back to Virginia together—*
> *get rearrested—*
> *that might be a good way*
> *to get this back in the courts.*

This guy is completely nuts.
Mildred grabbed hold of my hand
real tight—
like she thought I'd get up and walk out.

# MILDRED

Mr. Cohen tells us it's complicated.

A chill makes me pull my sweater closed.
I nod. Complicated?

The first thing we have to do,
he says,
is find a way to get our case
back in the courts.

While he's flipping through a stack of papers,
he's talking—he's saying
our case was heard five years ago.
We should have brought it to him
then—within 120 days
of our sentencing.

Then he laughs and says,
 "But I wasn't even in law school yet,
 five years ago.
 Let me think about how to get this in the courts—
 find a hook—
 and I'll call you. I think we can win this.
 It's an important case,
 Mr. and Mrs. Loving."
Important.
I nod again.

# RICHARD

Why is it SO DIFFICULT?
We just want to go home.

# MILDRED

Waiting
isn't easy.
We just want a telephone call to come and say,
        "Okay, you can go back home."

What we do get is a call
from Mr. Cohen
saying he found the hook.
He found another old case,
which a lawyer reopened
because it was
"still in the breast of the court."

That's what they do—
find old cases that some other lawyer won,
and use that as an argument
for what they want
to do.
What we want to do is
get the case back in the courts.

Mr. Cohen says our "suspended sentence"
means our case is not finished.
It's suspended, floating out there—
"still in the breast of the court."

Mr. Cohen says he filed a motion to ask Judge Bazile
"to vacate judgment"—
that is, change his mind.
Mr. Cohen says our sentence is
"cruel and unusual punishment"—
that our
"banishment"
violates the right to be married
under the 14th Amendment.

I think back to high school civics class,
try to remember the
14th Amendment of the U.S. Constitution.
At the time
I didn't think it had anything to do
with me.

Mr. Cohen says
he'll get back to us soon—
just as soon as he hears from Judge Leon Bazile.

Please please PLEASE,
Mr. Judge Bazile,
call Mr. Cohen and
say we can come home.
PLEASE.
It's so simple.
Just a phone call.

# THE RIGHTS OF A FREE PEOPLE

## NOVEMBER 1963

**BERNIE COHEN** was a young lawyer on fire. He knew the Lovings' case was important—he even loved their name, Loving, which described both the couple and the heart of the case.

The Lovings had pleaded guilty at their first trial. To avoid a prison sentence, they opted for Judge Bazile's offer of a suspended sentence. But that suspension—that pause—made the matter still under Judge Bazile's jurisdiction—or still "in the breast of the court."

Bernie Cohen filed a motion in Judge Bazile's Circuit Court of Caroline County to vacate the conviction—to annul or render void Judge Bazile's previous conviction of the Lovings and their suspended sentence of 1959.

In his motion, Cohen wrote that banishment for twenty-five years is **"CRUEL AND UNUSUAL PUNISHMENT"** and that the equal protection clause of the 14th Amendment of the U.S. Constitution protected the right to marry, which is a fundamental right of a free people.

In the course of his brief, Cohen contended that to keep the races from "mixing" requires segregation—and segregation was **ILLEGAL**.

*continued*

# 14ᵀᴴ AMENDMENT

"**Section 1.** All persons born or naturalized in the United States, and subject to the jurisdiction thereof, are citizens of the United States and of the state wherein they reside. No state shall make or enforce any law which shall abridge the privileges or immunities of citizens of the United States; nor shall any state deprive any person of life, liberty, or property, without **due process** of law; nor deny to any person within its jurisdiction the **equal protection** of the laws."

The 14ᵗʰ Amendment was ratified July 9, 1868, following the 13ᵗʰ Amendment, which abolished slavery and was ratified in 1865.

# RICHARD

I don't reckon we're ever
going to hear from those men.
I don't hold much hope.
They talk and talk and
then they forget about you
'cause they just talk talk TALKIN'
to someone else.
Just talk.
I told Millie to forget them.

# 1964

"It shall be . . . unlawful . . . to discriminate against any individual . . . because of such individual's race, color, religion, sex, or national origin." —CIVIL RIGHTS ACT OF 1964

**July 1964** *President Lyndon Johnson signs the Civil Rights Act into law*

# MILDRED

Waiting.
Mr. Cohen said he'll call me
when he hears from Judge Bazile.
I stopped calling him and asking.
The answer is always no.
I decided a letter might be better.

*Dear Mr. Cohen,*

*Hope that you remember us.*
*You took our case.*
*We haven't heard anything*
*in so long, we've given up hope.*

*Sincerely,*
*Mr. and Mrs. Loving*

# RICHARD

We had an appointment with the lawyers
in their Washington, D.C., office.
I said to Mr. Cohen,

> *Can't you just go see Judge Bazile?*
> *We're Americans.*
> *He has no right to say No.*

# MILDRED

Mr. Cohen says,
      "Mr. and Mrs. Loving,
      we're working on the case.
      We have to wait on Judge Bazile.
      I know this is frustrating.
      He's clearly stalling—
      perhaps he's hoping to retire
      before he has to rule on your case.
      But I don't think that will happen.
      It's not over.
      Please be patient."

He introduces us to Mr. Hirschkop,
who is also working on our case.
Mr. Hirschkop says,
      "I've requested
      a temporary restraining order
      against enforcement
      of your original sentence."
He calls it an
"off-the-record truce."

Richard and I sit
in their itty-bitty office
in Washington, D.C.,
wondering what this means
exactly.

1964

**November 1964** *Mildred and Richard Loving meet with ACLU lawyers Bernard Cohen and Philip Hirschkop*

Richard is slouched low in his chair.
He has nothing to say.
They can see he's disgusted.
When they leave the room
Richard takes hold of my hand.

When they return,
he's still holding my hand.

The lawyers say they'll call us
when they get word.

We've heard this before
but I know these men
are working hard for us.
I remind myself that it's complicated.

We just don't know why
it takes so long.
It's so simple.
We want to go home.
I want to call
President Johnson
and for him to say
Mr. and Mrs. Loving,
You may go home.

# MILDRED

Mr. Hirschkop calls.
      "Mrs. Loving, I have good news.
      You and Mr. Loving may return—
      not to Caroline County—
      but to one of the nearby counties—
      Essex or King and Queen County,
      as long as
      political tension doesn't mount."

That is the "off-the-record truce."

He says we won't be bothered.
He says, "If it gets too hot
      you'll have a week
      to leave Virginia."
He says, "If there's some problem
      and you get arrested
      we'll get you out of jail
      within an hour."

He advises us to keep our apartment
in Washington
just in case we need
to leave Virginia
quickly.

While I'm waiting for Richard to come home
and tell him the news
I start packing the children's clothes.
Laura stands in the doorway
and smiles at me.

# RICHARD

I found us a nice farmhouse to let
on the edge of King and Queen County
close to home—
just a few miles from Passing Road, Central Point,
Caroline County.
It's isolated.
You can see the road for a piece—
see if anyone's driving up.

And I found work in Washington,
good pay—
$5 an hour.
The lawyers say this is important—
my working in Washington.
It's part of hiding.
My paycheck comes from Washington, D.C.,
where we're supposed
to be living.

It's kind of crazy,
still drive back and forth
eating up $35 a week in gas.
But it's nice to be near home.
It makes Millie
a far sight
happier.
And every now and then
she laughs—
that beautiful laugh that I love so much.

# MILDRED

The children play outside.
Richard has made them a tire swing.
When it's warm enough
they can run barefoot and not
worry about broken glass in the streets.
But today they put on shoes.

No more city sounds.
No more sirens and honking.
Instead
owls hoot at night,
crows caw in daytime,
cardinals flash through the yard.

The farmhouse comes with cats
and Daddy loaned us Jack.
Sidney chases the black cat,
and Jack, barking to high heaven,
chases Sidney.
Don chases Jack.
Everyone is laughing.
Maybe even all that barking
is Jack
laughing.

Peggy helps me gather sticks
for the stove.
Richard is at work.
I feel a huge weight
lift off my shoulders—
like I've been carrying
a big ole boulder around
for six years—
and I just now
let it roll off.

I do keep my eye on the road
and get ready to gather the children
if the sheriff drives up.
I remind myself,
if we get arrested,
they'll get us out in one hour.
Five hours at the most,
they say.
Living here
is worth that risk.

I enroll Sidney in school,
across the line in Essex County
because it's the closest to
our farmhouse.
When I go to pick him up
after school
the Essex County sheriff rolls up, says,

"They might look the other way in King and Queen,
but here in Essex,
we ever see you
together with your husband,
we'll arrest you."

I'll find a school in King and Queen.
We'll have to drive farther to get him there.
Maybe we'll get bus service—
but there aren't always buses
for colored kids.

# "ALMIGHTY GOD CREATED THE RACES WHITE, BLACK, YELLOW, MALAY, AND RED"

## JANUARY 1965

A federal three-judge panel convened to consider Cohen and Hirschkop's motion—whether Virginia's anti-miscegenation laws were constitutional and whether they could be enforced by the State. The judges heard the case on **DECEMBER 28, 1964**. The three judges declined to rule on Virginia's law, saying the issue might still be resolved in the Virginia State Court.

However, the spokesman for the three-judge panel, Judge Butznor, gave Judge Bazile and the State of Virginia a maximum of 90 days to "render an opinion" or the case would go to Federal Court. The threat to the Lovings of being imprisoned required the Virginia court to answer without delay.

## Finally, in January of 1965, Leon Bazile made his ruling.

Citing cases from the 1820s—when slavery was legal—Judge Leon Bazile found that whipping, selling, or exiling people was not cruel or unusual punishment. Neither was sterilizing a defendant. Citing another case from the nineteenth century, also dated 40 years prior to the abolition of slavery, he found that what did constitute cruel and unusual punishment was a person being burned at the stake, crucified, or broken on the wheel (a torture device from the Middle Ages).

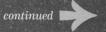

*continued*

In addition to citing century-old cases, Judge Leon Bazile made his own statement. He wrote:

"ALMIGHTY GOD CREATED THE RACES WHITE, BLACK, YELLOW, MALAY, AND RED AND HE PLACED THEM ON SEPARATE CONTINENTS. AND BUT FOR THE INTERFERENCE WITH HIS ARRANGEMENT THERE WOULD BE NO CAUSE FOR SUCH MARRIAGES. THE FACT THAT HE SEPARATED THE RACES SHOWS THAT HE DID NOT INTEND FOR THE RACES TO MIX."

# MILDRED

Judge Bazile did not change his mind.
He says Richard and I
committed a most serious crime.
We'll be known as felons
for the rest of our lives.

Mr. Cohen reads me
the judge's closing statement
over the phone.
I'm trying to sort it out.

God put each race of people on their own continent?
And meant them to stay there?
Didn't Judge Bazile go to school?
Didn't he learn that God put the Indians
on the America continent?
Cherokee? Rappahannock?
And then the white settlers arrived
and stole this land from the "red" people.
White people stole black people from the "black" continent.

Just WHO is guilty?
Didn't that judge go to school?

# RICHARD

Millie is right angry.
But the lawyers said they expected to lose.
They said the fight was not over.

They said this to us in their office.
I took up Millie's hand and she calmed down.
All I could say to Mr. Cohen and Mr. Hirschkop was,
      *Sure do appreciate the job,*
'cause I know they tried.

They said,
      *Go back to Washington for safety*
      *while we make the appeal.*

So we closed up the farmhouse,
moved back in with Alex and Laura,
upstairs in their house.
We apologized to them,
but what could we do?

# RICHARD

One hot night Ray, Percy, and me
were working under the oak tree
at Ray's—
put my V8 in the '62 Ford,
painted her black,
named her Delonoa,
painted her number—
ONE.

Millie was in the house with Annamae,
the kids were at her parents'.
'Round about midnight, the girls came out,
went back inside.
One o'clock in the morning,
girls came out, went back in.
Two o'clock, girls came out again.
They went back inside.
We just weren't done working.

I had something to say.
Finally, I said to Ray and Percy,

> *For the first time I live and work in the same place—*
> *Washington, D.C.—*
> *but years of going back and forth*
> *between Caroline County*
> *and Washington, D.C.—*
> *I got more experience*
> *driving than anyone.*

We all laughed
but they said, *Okay.*
　　　*You drive this one.*
　　　*You race in Parnassus.*

So come the weekend,
I'm lined up at the start
against Brian in his red Chevy—
the man to beat.
I'm pressin' on the gas,
my foot antsy on the clutch,
the Christmas tree, red,
blinks right down the line—
red, red, red, orange,
GREEN—
up with the clutch and I'm off,
just hangin' on to that steering wheel,
everything rattlin' and roarin'
YOWWWWW.
I am neck 'n' neck
with the red Chevy,
sweating hard,
I inch ahead.

Damned if I don't win.

I bring home the trophy—
we all been collecting plenty over time
and we divide them up—
this one's clearly
MINE.

# MILDRED

I scream alongside Annamae
on the sidelines.
I scream the whole heat.
I scream till I have no voice.

It feels SO good to win.

# MILDRED

The children are in school.
I look through the grimy window
at clothes hung on the line,
the garbage lining the street.
I long for the farmhouse
or better yet—
Passing Road—
living next door to my mother and father,
just down the road
from Richard's parents—
and ALWAYS I long for the songs of many birds
at the edge of the woods.

I long to hear Richard laugh.
It seems he hardly laughs
anymore.
Except when he's racing.
Racing is as much part of our life
in Virginia
as the creeks
the birds
the trees.

We celebrated Daddy's eighty-first birthday
this year.
He's not going to live forever.
Either are Twilley or Lola.
Or Mama, for that matter.
I know all of them could use our help.

I don't know when we'll hear
from our lawyers.
I hardly ever bring it up with Richard.
And the night I do,
I'm right sorry I did.
He plops down on the couch,
elbows on his knees,
drops his head
into his hands.

We just want to go home.
Please, Lord,
let us go HOME.

# "RACIAL INTEGRITY" AND "THE CORRUPTION OF BLOOD"

## JANUARY 1965 TO MARCH 1966

After losing the case in the district court of Caroline County, Bernie Cohen and Phil Hirschkop appealed to the Virginia Supreme Court of Appeals, asserting that the court had erred in not upholding the Lovings' equal protection right allowed by the 14th Amendment.

The lawyers argued that the right to marry was **FUNDAMENTAL**. If that right is restricted due to race, isn't that an unlawful infringement of one's liberty? What if the law stated you *must* marry someone of a different race? They said the state shouldn't interfere.

The lawyers further contended that the couple's sentence was **UNCONSTITUTIONAL**.

Knowing that Virginia's high court was a conservative body, Cohen and Hirschkop assumed they would lose the appeal. They did.

In **MARCH 1966**, Virginia sustained its anti-miscegenation laws—there would be no intermarrying. In its verdict, the Virginia Supreme Court of Appeals referred to its decision of the decade before, *Naim v. Naim*, in which it ruled that it was within the powers of the state "to preserve the racial integrity of its citizens," and to prevent "the corruption of blood."

However, presiding Judge Harry Carrico **DID MODIFY** the Lovings' sentence, saying the Lovings could return to Virginia together as long as they did not "cohabit" or sleep together overnight.

Carrico showed further compassion for the couple and "stayed" their sentence, giving them time to appeal the case to the highest court in the land.

# RICHARD

After waiting another year—
more like fourteen months—
they lost that case.
Is that four now?
They called for another.

The lawyers sure are excited
for losing.
They called us into Washington
and asked us to speak
to the reporters.
They poked microphones in our faces.

The cameras were rolling.
I just wanted to be home,
but I answered
their questions.

> *Have you thought about other people?*
> *Do you want to be the ones to change the law?*
> *Why did you take this to court?*
>
> *Yes, we have thought about other people*
> *but we are not doing it*
> *just because someone had to do it*
> *and we wanted to be the ones . . .*
> *We are doing it for us—*
> *because we want to live here.*

# MILDRED

Shoot.
After waiting and waiting
we lose in the highest court
in the state of Virginia.
The lawyers,
they expected that.

But Judge Carrico agreed with our lawyers.
He said that our first sentence was
cruel and unusual punishment—
six years of not being able
to travel home together to see
our families.
I'm glad he sees that.

And now our case can go
to the U.S. Supreme Court.

And while our lawyers
get ready for this next part of our case—
they say our sentence is
*stayed.*
Which means Richard and I can return
to our farmhouse
and live together in Virginia
and no one can
arrest us.

It's hard to believe.
Just maybe we'll sleep
a little easier,
knowing that no sheriff
can drive up to our house,
walk right in,
and go shining lights in our eyes
in the middle of the night.

And then Mr. Cohen says
someone could make a mistake
and the sheriff might still try
to arrest us.

I'm scared of Sheriff Brooks.
You never know what he'll do.
Anyway,
if we get arrested,
we'll call Mr. Cohen
and he'll get us right out.
He promises.
That's what I understand.

Mr. Cohen says
Judge Leon Bazile has done us a real nice favor
making that racist statement.
         "The Almighty God placed
         the races on their own continents . . ."
Indeed!

That business made me feel
the kind of wild anger I felt
when I was a child.

Mr. Cohen and Mr. Hirschkop
care that Richard and I
are tired of all this,
that we're struggling with money,
that we've paid out so much for Richard's gas money,
and he's been gone so long each day—
but being home
will be wonderful.

Clearly, they are excited
about taking our case to the very top.

And then we go outside where the newsmen
are all gathered.
For the camera, I say,
            "If we do win, we'll be helping a lot of people."

We pick up the kids
at my parents' house and go to the farmhouse.
I walk out into the field with
Sidney, Don, and Peggy.
I watch them run and yell,
their voices
muffled by the wind.

A group of big black crows
stands around on the stubbly land—
until the children run at them.
The crows take off,
float on the wind.
Some try to make their way
into the wind, but the wind
won't allow it.
The crows seem to say,
I want to go over there
but the wind says, No, I want you here.
So they let the wind carry them
real graceful on outstretched wings.
I think,
that's like our life.
We're those crows.
The wind is casting us around—
go live here,
now you can live there,
now get on over there.
You can't control the wind.

They say we're making progress.

# FREEDOM OF THE INDIVIDUAL VERSUS THE RIGHT OF THE STATE

## MAY 1966

Bernie Cohen and Phil Hirschkop spent hours in law libraries researching and composing their appeal to the U.S. Supreme Court. The two young lawyers were further advised by the **NATIONAL CIVIL LIBERTIES UNION**.

More experienced lawyers were added to their team, including Mel Wulf and David Carliner, then William Zabel, Arthur Berney, and Marvin Karpatkin.

The team of lawyers' number-one question addressed whether the Virginia courts had provided the Lovings with equal protection as is promised by the **14ᵀᴴ AMENDMENT**.

Their second question addressed whether the Lovings were denied due process of the law; whether the state could interfere with an individual's choice of a mate.

*continued*

This was a case of *freedom of the individual* versus *the right of the state*—a huge case for such young lawyers.

Phil Hirschkop, only two years out of law school, was not yet eligible to request that a case be heard in the U.S. Supreme Court. Bernie Cohen, three years out of law school, was barely eligible to request the case, which he did. Hirschkop and Cohen filed their notice of appeal to the U.S. Supreme Court on May 31, 1966. On December 12 of that year, the U.S. Supreme Court accepted the case. This in itself was a big step, as the Supreme Court takes only one out of several hundred cases put before it.

**THE HEARING WAS SET FOR APRIL 10, 1967.**

# RICHARD

Tomorrow our case gets heard in Washington.
Mr. Cohen asked us to attend.
We're not going.
We just want to be left alone
and live our lives.
I know this is the last court.
You can't go higher
than the U.S. Supreme Court.

When Mr. Cohen asked for a statement,
I said,

>Tell the Court I love my wife
>and it is just unfair that I can't live with her
>in Virginia.

While we were in the city talking
some white-hooded creeps burned a cross at Jeters' house.
The Klan.
Once that would have screwed up my head.
Now, it feels just about normal.
I never thought my life would be like this.

We went home to the farmhouse
and I drank a beer.
And another.
And ANOTHER.
No matter how much I drank
I couldn't get drunk.

# MILDRED

Richard and Peggy
work on a puzzle together.
Richard lifts Peggy off his lap.
Without her daddy
she goes back to dressing
paper dolls with magazine cut-outs.
Richard takes a beer
from the icebox and goes outside.
The boys surround him.
Usually he'd play ball with them
or he'd get them huddled
under the hood of his car.
Instead he pats them each on the head
and walks out toward the sunset.

The court has four months
before it has to rule
on our case.
It's a fine thing we're
good at
waiting.

# EQUAL JUSTICE
# UNDER LAW

  **APRIL TO JUNE 1967**

The State of Virginia, in prosecuting the Lovings, had been looking at its Racial Integrity Act of 1924, which denied the right for a white person to marry a colored person.

Cohen and Hirschkop suggested that since this 1924 legislation *did* allow Negroes to marry those of other races, Negroes were subject to losing *their* racial purity. The Act enforced only the "purity" of the white race.

That inconsistency of guarding the purity of one race but not another implied that one race was superior to another. The lawyers said this law was a "relic of slavery." To do anything but overturn Virginia's case against the Lovings was "fostering racial prejudice" and promoted the "myth that Negroes are innately inferior to whites."

In his Appeal to the U.S. Supreme Court, Bernie Cohen had argued, "marriage is such a basic, fundamental, and natural right and the choice of a mate must be left to one's own desires and conscience." Marriage should be **"BEYOND THE ARBITRARY GRASP OF THE STATE."**

*continued*

The defendant, the State of Virginia, argued that the 14<sup>th</sup> Amendment did not cover intermarriage. North Carolina joined them, in an "amicus brief"—a statement intended to assist the court—defending the "southern way of life."

The Lovings' lawyers said the Lovings should be able to raise their children where they themselves had been raised, in their home state. Furthermore, the children should not have to live "under the stigma of bastardy" or illegitimacy. Upholding the Virginia laws amounted to **"LEGALIZED PREJUDICE"** and relegated the Negro to second-class citizenship.

The U.S. Supreme Court, in 1967, consisted of eight associate justices and **CHIEF JUSTICE EARL WARREN**. After deliberating in chambers, the justices' votes were unanimous.

ON JUNE 12, 1967,
CHIEF JUSTICE WARREN
RETURNED TO THE PODIUM
AND PROCLAIMED, SIMPLY,
"JUDGMENT REVERSED."

# MILDRED

We WON.
Mr. Cohen and Mr. Hirschkop are on the phone.
They ask us to come
to the press conference
at their office
in Alexandria—
right here in Virginia.
We don't have to pretend
we live in Washington.
We can go—
TOGETHER—
to their Virginia office.

I put my hand over the phone
and ask Richard
about driving to Alexandria.

He frowns and says, "No.
        It's time they leave us alone."

I say to Mr. Cohen,
        "Thank you for everything,
        but I don't think so."

He says,
        "Mrs. Loving,
        this is important.
        I think it would be good
        for America to hear you speak."

I cover the phone again and say,

"Richard, Mr. Cohen thinks this is important.
We can take the kids to Garnet's."

He nods.

"Okay, Mr. Cohen, we'll be there
as soon as we can."

But it's still a few hours away.

# RICHARD

I drove fast.
Maybe so I could get it
all over with
so we could live
peacefully—
the sooner the better.
Millie was excited—
that made me happy.

At the press conference, I said,
> *We're just really overjoyed.*
> *I didn't really expect to win.*
> *This has been going on for nine long years.*

When they asked if I had been ready to give up,
I said, *I would do it again.*
> *If we lost, I'd file another suit*
> *in another five years.*
> *This is what I want.*

They asked,
> *Who do you think your children should marry?*

> *I think I'd leave that up to them.*
> *Let them decide for themselves.*

Plans? *Yes. My wife and I plan*
> *to go ahead and build a new house now—*
> *next to her parents' house.*

How does it feel?

It feels—
it's hard to believe.
For the first time I can put my arm around her
and publicly call her my wife.

And that's what I do.

# MILDRED

At the press conference, I say,
     "I feel free now.
     It was a great burden.
     Yes, I thought the Court would rule in our favor.
     No, our neighbors have not been hostile.
     No, we do not bear a grudge
     against the State of Virginia.
     Yes, the children are six, seven, and eight.
     No, they're not aware of the case.
     It's best to leave them out of it."

Somewhere in there I start crying, but not hot angry tears.
Tears stream down my cheeks
because so much has happened.
Nine years' worth of tears
slide down my face.

Mr. Cohen says to the newsman,
     "We hope we have put to rest the last vestiges of
     racial discrimination
     in Virginia and all over the country."

When the cameras are gone
I begin thanking Mr. Cohen
and to my surprise
and maybe his too
I lift my arms and hug him.
The same with Mr. Hirschkop.
I am filled with joy.
Richard and I can go home now
and our family can live in peace.

# RICHARD

I was working on the car
in our yard—
well, what will be our yard.
We're at the Jeter house again
until we can build our own house.

A car drove past slow enough.
I looked up—
Sheriff Brooks in his
black Ford truck,
that dog in the back—
driving down our road,
Passing Road.

What does he think he's gonna do?
Make his own law.
He lost.
He lost but GOOD.

I laughed and got back
under the hood
of the Ford.

Millie walked up,
leaned on me,
looked at the engine
and said something about
how clean it looked.
I wiped my hands on a rag,

draped it around her,
both of us laughing soft.
We rocked for a moment.

*There,* I said.
>    *We'll build the house there—*
>    *pretty close to where I caught*
>    *your home run ball.*

She looked at me funny.

>    *Bean, don't you remember?*
>    *I was there with your brothers,*
>    *caught your fly ball coming through*
>    *the apple tree, there.*
>    *You was mad as a hornet—*
>    *thought you was going to kill me.*

I could tell she was working hard to remember.
She said, *Yep, I think I do remember.*

Can't tell if she really did.
Don't matter.

I smiled and said,
>    *Couldn't have done this without you.*
She laughed at that.
I laughed.
She said,
>    *This whole*
>    *thing brought us closer together,*
>    *I think.*
>    *Do you?*

>    *Yeah, I think so.*

# MILDRED

I'd like to forget a lot
about the last nine years.
All, but what is precious to me—
my family—
our kids growing up
with their daddy
and me.

I take off my shoes
and feel the grass
soft underfoot.
I don't mind the sticks and the pebbles.
I just feel the give of the soil
and the cool of the grass.

I follow my children through the trees
to the creek.
Sidney has waded in,
already fallen.
I think he did that on purpose.
Don is laughing at him,
so Sidney pulls him in too.

They're laughing so hard
no one needs pushing.
They can't even stand back up.
Peggy is scooping for tadpoles,
just like Garnet and I did
as kids.

I spot blackberries at the edge of the wood
and eat a few.
I show my children.
They pick some,
load their pockets.

Sidney points out a sparrow
and a nest
filled with hungry babies.

Next weekend my brothers and Garnet
will come by
and some neighbor folk—
maybe.
It will be Father's Day.

Mama will boil a chicken or two.
I'll cook up some cabbage.
Maybe Mama will make a pie.

We'll all sit around the table,
join hands,
and thank God.

# RICHARD PERRY LOVING (1933–1975)

# MILDRED DELORES JETER LOVING (1939–2008)

After nine years of exile, Richard built the family a house where they lived happily for eight years. In 1975, Richard and Mildred were driving home from the Bowling Green carnival on Sparta Road, when they were hit by a car driven by a drunk driver. Mildred was blinded in one eye and Richard was killed. Ray Green, driving behind them, saw it happen. Mildred lived out the rest of her life surrounded by family and friends in the house Richard built on Passing Road, Caroline County, Virginia. She died of pneumonia in 2008 at the age of sixty-eight.

In her obituary in the *Washington Post* (May 6, 2008), Mildred is quoted as having said,

"We each loved each other and got married. We are not marrying the state. The law should allow a person to marry anyone he wants."

# LOVING VS. VIRGINIA
# TIME LINE

**DECEMBER 6, 1865**—13th Amendment ratified into U.S. Constitution—slavery is abolished

**JULY 9, 1868**—14th Amendment ratified into U.S. Constitution

**1896**—*Plessy v Ferguson*—separate but equal idea becomes the law of the land

**1924**—Racial Integrity Act of Virginia enacted

**1954**—*Brown v Board of Education*—U.S. Supreme Court rules that all schools must desegregate

**FEBRUARY 25, 1956**—Virginia's "Massive Resistance" begins; county officials close schools rather than integrate

**SEPTEMBER 1957**—Little Rock Nine, Arkansas—nine African American students were prevented from attending Little Rock Central High School on September 4 by order of Arkansas Governor Orval Faubus; the nine students were admitted September 25 by order of President Dwight D. Eisenhower

**JUNE 2, 1958**—Richard Loving and Mildred Jeter marry in Washington, D.C., and go home to Virginia

**JULY 11, 1958**—Lovings are arrested in Central Point for miscegenation

**SEPTEMBER 1958**—Little Rock, Arkansas—Governor Faubus closes Little Rock high schools for the year to prevent segregated attendance

**JANUARY 6, 1959**—Lovings tried, found guilty, and sentenced by the Caroline County Circuit Court

**JANUARY 19, 1959**—Virginia's school-closing law is found to violate the State Constitution

**MARCH 28, 1959**—Lovings violate parole and are rearrested, but charges are dropped

**FEBRUARY 1960**—Sit-in at Woolworth's lunch counter in North Carolina sparks wave of similar protests

**MAY 1961**—"Freedom Riders" become active in the Deep South

**APRIL 16, 1963**—Martin Luther King Jr. writes his "Letter from Birmingham Jail"

**AUGUST 28, 1963**—Martin Luther King Jr. leads the March on Washington

**NOVEMBER 6, 1963**—Bernard Cohen of the ACLU files motion to vacate judgment and set aside the sentence in the *Commonwealth of Virginia v Loving and Jeter* case

**OCTOBER 28, 1964**—When their case is still not decided, the Lovings, aided by the ACLU, file a class-action suit in the U.S. District Court for the Eastern District of Virginia

**JANUARY 1965**—Judge Leon Bazile denies the move to vacate judgment with his famous "The Almighty God . . ." opinion

**FEBRUARY 11, 1965**—Three-judge district court makes decision to allow Lovings to present their claim to the Virginia Supreme Court of Appeals

**MARCH 1966**—Virginia Supreme Court, headed by Judge Carrico, sustains the anti-miscegenation laws in the Lovings' case

**MAY 31, 1966**—The Lovings, aided by the ACLU, appeal the decision to the U.S. Supreme Court

**DECEMBER 12, 1966**—U.S. Supreme Court accepts the *Loving v Virginia* case

**JUNE 12, 1967**—U.S. Supreme Court overturns the Lovings' convictions in unanimous decision

**JUNE 1967**—The Lovings return home to Passing Road, Central Point, Caroline County, Virginia

**JUNE 29, 1975**—Richard dies at forty-one years old after being hit by a drunk driver

**MAY 2, 2008**—Mildred dies of pneumonia, surrounded by her remaining family, at sixty-eight years old

# BIBLIOGRAPHY

## INTERVIEWS

All interviews conducted by the author.

Buirsky, Nancy. Phone interview, June 15, 2012.

Coleman, Cleo(patra). Phone interview, March 6, 2013.

Coleman, Sandy. In-person interview, July 18, 2012.

Green, Raymond, with John Coleman, Buster Fortune, and fourth man. In-person interview, July 19, 2012.

Jeter, Otha. Phone interviews, July 18, 2012; February 22, 2013; May 1, 2013.

Jeter, Otha. In-person interviews, July 20, 2012; July 21, 2012.

Jeter, Lewis. Phone interviews, May 21, 2012; June 14, 2012; July 21, 2012; February 16, 2013.

Jett, David (Tappahannock Historical Society). Phone interview, March 6, 2013.

Johnson, Homer, with Jerry Chinault. In-person interview, July 19, 2012.

Lemons, Nokomis, and Wallace Lemons. Phone interview, July 20, 2012.

# WRITTEN MATERIAL

American Civil Liberties Union. *Feature Press Service.* March 15, 1965.

Booker, Simon. "The Couple That Rocked the Courts." *Ebony,* September 1967: 78–84.

Buirsky, Nancy, and Susie Ruth Powell. *The Loving Story.* DVD. Directed by Nancy Buirski. Augusta Films, The National Endowment for the Humanities, 2011.

Caroline County (Va.) *Commonwealth versus Richard Perry Loving and Mildred Delores Jeter, 1958–1966.* Caroline County (Va.) Reel 79. Local government records collection, Caroline County Court Records. The Library of Virginia, Richmond, Virginia 23219.

Coleman, Arica L. *That the Blood Stay Pure: African Americans, Native Americans, and the Predicament of Race and Identity in Virginia.* Bloomington, IN. Indiana University Press, 2013.

Hampton, Henry, and Steve Fayer. *Voices of Freedom: An Oral History of the Civil Rights Movement from the 1950s through the 1980s.* New York: Bantam, 1990.

Kurland, Philip B., and Gerhard Casper, eds. *Landmark Briefs and Arguments of the Supreme Court of the United States: Constitutional Law.* Arlington, VA: University Publications of America, 1975.

*LIFE.* "The Crime of Being Married." March 18, 1966: 85–91.

Nagai, Tyrone. "Multiracial Identity and the U.S. Census." ProQuest Discovery Guides, January 2010.

Newbeck, Phyl. *Virginia Hasn't Always Been for Lovers: Interracial Marriage Bans and the Case of Richard and Mildred Loving.* Carbondale, IL: Southern Illinois University Press, 2004.

Margolick, David. "Mixed Marriage's 25th Anniversary of Legality." *New York Times*, June 12, 1992.

Martin, Douglas. "Mildred Loving, Who Battled Ban on Mixed-Race Marriage, Dies at 68." *New York Times*, May 6, 2008.

*New York Times*. "Virginia Suit Scores Mixed Marriage Ban." July 30, 1966.

*The Pointer*. Union High School Yearbooks. Caroline County, VA, 1952–1956, 1958–1969.

Pratt, Robert A. "Crossing the Color Line: A Historical Assessment and Personal Narrative of *Loving v. Virginia*." *Howard Law Journal* 41 (Winter 1998): 229–45.

Ryden, Hope, and Abbot Mill. [12-mm footage of the Loving family in their home and with lawyers.] Robert Drew & Associates, 1965.

Sickels, Robert J. *Race, Marriage, and the Law*. Albuquerque, NM: University of New Mexico Press, 1972.

Wallenstein, Peter. *Tell the Court I Love My Wife: Race, Marriage, and Law—An American History*. New York: Palgrave Macmillan, 2002.

White, Jean M. "Court Overturns Virginia's Ban on Mixed Marriages." *Washington Post*, June 13, 1967.

Wingfield, Marshall. *A History of Caroline County Virginia: From its Formation in 1727 to 1924. Compiled from Original Records and Authoritative Sources and Profusely Illustrated*. [To which is Appended "A Discourse of Virginia" by Edward Maria Wingfield.] Richmond, VA: Trevvet Christian & Co., 1924.

# IMAGE CREDITS

The author has made every attempt to locate the rights holders of all materials used in this book. If further information is available, please contact the publisher.

Page 2: [Emancipation Proclamation] Library of Congress

Page 4: [Racial Integrity Act] State Library of Virginia

Page 8: [White classroom] Photo by J. E. Schrock, courtesy of Topeka and Shawnee County Public Library

Page 9: [Black classroom] Library of Congress, Jack Delano photographer

Page 84: [Black boys] Library of Congress, Thomas J. O'Halloran photographer

Page 85: [Elizabeth Eckford] Lloyd Dinkins/Commercial Appeal/Landov

Page 147: [No Child Is Free Until All Are Free] Photographs and Prints Division, Schomburg Center for Research in Black Culture, The New York Public Library, Astor, Lenox and Tilden Foundations; photographer unknown

Pages 162–163: [Race Mixing Is Communist] Library of Congress, John T. Bledsoe photographer

Pages 164–165: [Black boy watches demonstrators] Library of Congress, John T. Bledsoe photographer

Pages 166–167: [lunch counter] Magnum, Danny Lyon photographer

Page 169: [Freedom Riders burning bus] Birmingham Civil Rights Institute, Joe Postiglione photographer

Page 183: [March on Washington] Library of Congress, Warren K. Leffler photographer

Pagea 196–197: [LBJ signs Civil Rights Act] LBJ Library, Cecil Stoughton photographer

Page 201: [Cohen & Hirschkop] copyright Grey Villet Estate

## TEXT CREDITS

Pages 2–3: "Long View: Negro" by Langston Hughes
*Paper:* "Long View: Negro" from THE COLLECTED POEMS OF LANGSTON HUGHES by Langston Hughes, edited by Arnold Rampersad with David Roessel, Associate Editor, copyright © 1994 by the Estate of Langston Hughes. Used by permission of Alfred A. Knopf, an imprint of the Knopf Doubleday Publishing Group, a division of Random House LLC. All rights reserved.
*Electronic:* Reprinted by permission of Harold Ober Associates Incorporated
Copyright © 1994 by the Estate of Langston Hughes

Pages 176 and 182: Excerpts from "Letter from Birmingham Jail" and "I Have a Dream" speech by Dr. Martin Luther King Jr. Reprinted by arrangement with The Heirs of the Estate of Martin Luther King Jr., c/o Writers House as agent for the proprietor New York, NY. Dream: © 1963 Dr. Martin Luther King Jr.

## QUOTE SOURCES

Page 9: "[A] segregationist is one who conscientiously believes . . ." George Wallace, Governor of Alabama. *U.S. News and World Report,* 1964.

Page 71: "Whether Virginia's high schools, which closed on a seg-
regated basis . . ."
Edward R. Murrow. CBS's TV documentary "Lost Class of 1959,"
January 21, 1959.

Page 84: "What good is it doing to force these situations . . ."
George Wallace, Governor of Alabama. *New York Times*, September 6,
1963.

Page 165: "In the name of the greatest people that have ever trod
this earth . . ."
George Wallace, Governor of Alabama. Inaugural Address,
January 14, 1963.

Page 194: U.S. Constitution. Amendment XIV, section 1.

Page 196: Civil Rights Act of 1964, Public Law 88-352,
78 Statute 241 (1964).

Pages 210 and 212: Loving v. Virginia, 388 United States
Supreme Court Reports 1 (1967).

Although the Supreme Court ruled on *Loving vs. Virginia* in 1967, it was many years before the remaining sixteen states that had anti-miscegenation laws struck those laws from their state constitutions.

The last anti-miscegenation law in the United States, in Alabama, was reversed in the year 2000.

# FROM THE ARTIST

When I was asked to illustrate Patricia Hruby Powell's wonderful telling of the Lovings' story, I was thrilled to be given the opportunity to depict such an important story, and excited to reference a style of illustrative reporting from the Lovings' time called visual journalism, pioneered by the artist Robert Weaver.

Leo Lionni, the famed illustrator and art director of *Fortune* magazine in the 1950s, was a driving force in the growth of visual journalism. He hired artists (including Weaver) to report on the magazine's stories through illustration. As it developed, visual journalism was often characterized by a loose, impromptu drawing style that allowed lines to overlap and preserved the informal feeling of sketches in the final composition.

I couldn't travel back to the days when Richard and Mildred fell in love, but I referenced Grey Villet's photographs of the Lovings from the *LIFE* magazine feature, as well as photographs from my mother's childhood in the '50s. (There are, unfortunately, no photographs of Mildred or Richard as children.) Then, without any preliminary sketches, I drew freely with a brush pen on paper at a scale twice the size of the book. The result is a collection of honest, energetic, and fluid illustrations that reflect, I hope, both the time and the journey that Richard and Mildred experienced together.

# ACKNOWLEDGMENTS

I am deeply indebted to the friends and family of Richard and Mildred Loving, who spoke to me about their early life in Caroline County—especially to Mildred's brothers Lewis Jeter and Otha Jeter—and to Ray Green, John Coleman, Buster Fortune, and everyone who hung out around the pickup truck behind Sparta Food Mart. And to Sandy Coleman, who kindly, enthusiastically directed me there. To David Jett, historian at Tappahannock Historical Society for all kinds of details. To Cleopatra Coleman, who told me about the one-room schoolhouses supported by the Black Baptist churches. To Nokomis and Wallace Lemons, who filled me in about the Rappahannock Nation. And to everyone who knew Mildred and Richard and encouraged me to tell the story.

Thanks to Nancy Buirski and her award-winning documentary, *The Loving Story*, and for directing me to Hope Ryden's 1960s film footage of the Loving family.

Thanks to Nadine Pinede, Candy Fleming, and Sari Boren for help in guiding me through what felt like a minefield of image searching, ownership, and permissions.

To my writing group and first readers: Elaine Bearden, Jessica Denhart, Sara Latta, Kara Laughlin, Marianne Malone, Alice McGinty, Mary Jessie Parker, Ruth Siburt, and Anne Wendler—y'all saw various versions of *Loving* and helped me scour it clean.

Thanks to Ragdale for the time and space to work.

To Melih Sener and Chantelle Hougland for reading and understanding the poem for two. And rereading, letting me tweak, commenting, rereading again, letting me hear, and helping me shape the poem.

To my editor, Melissa Manlove, for her vision, patience, brilliance, and friendship. This book would not have been if it weren't for Melissa. To my publisher, Ginee Seo, who suggested the book. And to the whole amazing, supportive Chronicle team, especially Jennifer Tolo Pierce, Marie Oishi, Lara Starr, Jaime Wong, Sally Kim, Taylor Norman, Binh Au, and Tera Killip.

And to Morgan Powell, forever, for just being one of the guys hanging around the pickup truck at the Sparta Road interview and for believing in me.